D0345762

The Yellow Room

Christopher Bowden

LANGTON & WOOD

Copyright © Christopher Bowden 2009
First published in 2009 by Langton & Wood
73 Alexandra Drive, London SE19 1AN
http://www.amolibros.com/bowden

Distributed by Gardners Books, 1 Whittle Drive, Eastbourne,
East Sussex, BN23 6QH
Tel: +44(0)1323 521555 | Fax: +44(0)1323 521666

The right of Christopher Bowden to be identified as the author
of the work has been asserted herein in accordance with the
Copyright, Designs and Patents Act 1988.

All rights reserved. This book is sold subject to the condition
that it sha   , resold,
hired out   er's prior
consent   that in
which it is   including
this cond   chaser.

All the char   emblance
to ac   ary.

Bri   a
A cata   the
British Library.

CITY OF LONDON LIBRARIES

CL 1079811 0

HJ	18-Sep-2009
GENERAL	£8.99
FICTION	BB

ISBN 978-0-9555067-1-0

Typeset by Amolibros, Milverton, Somerset
www.amolibros.co.uk
This book production has been managed by Amolibros
Printed and bound by T J International Ltd, Padstow, Cornwall, UK

Prologue

The Present

Jessica Tate ordered another cappuccino while she waited downstairs in Donatello's, the café near Leicester Square where she and Duncan had agreed to meet. She sighed and looked at her watch. He was late. That was unlike him. He was always on time, always. Still, it was only ten minutes or so. No use in worrying. It was probably nothing.

She pulled a book out of her bag, glanced at the picture on the front and the blurb on the back, and put it face down on the small circular table. She gazed at the glass roof above her, the straggling rain drops inching soundlessly towards the gutter. The drops caught the lightening sky, just visible beyond the damp stone balustrade and the trunks of towering plane trees.

She looked at her watch again, shifted in her chair and pulled at the ends of the dark brown hair falling from her shoulders. She leaned forward on the table and dragged the chair closer. It scraped horribly on the tiled floor. The desiccated couple at the next table glared over bags and packages and tutted in unison. Jessica reddened and reached for the saucer of sugar lumps. They were tightly wrapped in reproductions of Cubist paintings.

There's no point in what ifs, she reflected, as she placed one lump on top of another. It had to be faced. What's done is done and can't be undone. The leaning tower of lumps wobbled dangerously. How much simpler if she had put back what she found in her grandmother's cottage all those months ago, left things as they were, lying undisturbed. Brockley House would have remained a name unknown, a place unvisited, and she would have been none the wiser. But once she had set off down the road she needed to know where it led. And she wouldn't have met Duncan, either, would she? That was worth all the rest put together. Where was he?

Anyway, she thought, problems were there to be solved. She did not like ambiguity, uncertainty, loose ends. Perhaps it was her legal training, or maybe she just had the kind of mind that made her want to be a lawyer in the first place. And no one had been hurt, had they? Not really. Not much. Not yet.

She coaxed the last remaining Braque onto a wayward Picasso. It was a lump too far. The tower collapsed, sending cubes in all directions. The desiccated couple collected their bags and packages and huffed up the stairs to the street above. A slim man with sandy hair brushed past and patiently gathered the errant lumps.

"Sorry, I'm late," said Duncan Westwood, kissing Jessica warmly on the lips as she jumped up to meet him. She was too relieved to speak. He presented the sugar in cupped hands, like an offering. "Signal failure at Camden Town and a suspect container at Tottenham Court Road." He put the lumps in a pile on the table and sat down close beside her. His hair, she saw, was covered in a fine spray and the shoulders of his jacket were damp. He paused as Jessica's cappuccino arrived. Then he ordered an espresso for himself and said, "I was thinking about what you said last night. Are you sure you want to go through with this?"

Part One

Coronation Day 1953

Stanley Finch, caretaker of Brockley Village Hall, was stubbing out his cigarette in the chipped scallop shell that served as an ashtray when he heard a noise, almost a squeal, coming from the stage. At least, he thought he did. It was hard to tell above the hubbub coming from the Hall. He went down the corridor, freshly painted in brown and cream, past the open door of the dressing room, up the worn wooden steps and onto the back of the stage. As he fumbled for the light switch he knocked against a bank of bright red fire buckets filled alternately with sand and water. They swung creakily on brackets sprouting from the wall.

The brightly lit stage was completely bare. Finch crossed to the prompt corner on the other side and picked up the dog-eared copy of *Dandy Dick* lying under the chair. He flicked through the heavily annotated script and tossed it contemptuously onto the lumpy cushion covering the seat. He glanced towards the back of the stage, grunted and made for the heavy green curtains at the front. He parted them carefully, his stubbled chin rasping against the braided edge of the velvet, and looked into the body of the Hall.

It was decked with bunting and union jacks. At long tables covered in white cloths the children of Brockley were demolishing plates of sausage rolls, jam tarts and fairy cakes. They rocked excitedly on the faded canvas seats of the tubular metal chairs. They tapped their feet and scuffed their shoes against the wooden floor, neatly marked out as a badminton court. Impervious to noise and jelly, boy scouts in smart new uniforms brought round jugs of orange squash and lemonade to lubricate the ravening horde.

"Mum," wailed a small girl with red, white and blue ribbons in her hair. "Billy Smith done a wee in my Coronation mug." As an irate adult attempted to pounce, Billy laughed and crawled under the table. He was entirely obscured by the cloth.

"Bedlam," muttered Finch as the curtains fell gently to a close.

Twenty years ago the Hall was a barn. It was converted at the initiative of the Brockley Women's Institute, who found the local Reading Room too crowded for their monthly meetings. The proceeds of fêtes, whist drives and 'dramatic entertainments' over several years, together with a grant from the National Council of Social Service, raised enough to fund the conversion of the disused barn donated to the small Hampshire village by Sir Miles Brockley.

Finch had been working for Sir Miles up at the House in those days, doing the odd jobs and running repairs of which there never seemed to be a shortage. But the war had changed all that. After six years in the army he was not going to go back to that way of life, taking orders from toffs, thank you very much. It was not right.

Not any more. Mind you, Muriel, his wife, did for Lady Pamela two or three mornings a week. And her an earl's daughter into the bargain. He did not approve but every little helped.

Finch clumped back to the corridor. The door of the dressing room was now closed. He continued to the kitchen where Mrs Box, in charge of sandwiches, was rinsing lettuce in a vast ceramic sink. She scooped the lettuce into a colander, dried her hands roughly on a stained tea towel and turned unsteadily. "Shame about the rain," she said. "On today of all days."

Finch sat down with a grunt. "It may be a New Elizabethan Age but it's the same old weather."

She poured him a cup of tea from the big brown teapot lurking under its cosy on the scrubbed pine table. "People are saying Mount Everest should be called Mount Elizabeth in honour of our new Queen."

"Can't think why. It's not ours to call what we like. It wasn't even a Briton who made it to the top." He slurped his tea noisily.

"Well, the papers said Everest was British too. Whoever he was." She eased herself onto the other chair.

"Makes no difference."

"Are you coming to the sports on the recreation field? Lady Pamela is presenting the prizes."

"I'll be clearing up this place. Have you seen the state of the Hall?"

"But won't your May be competing in the sack race?"

"She's too old for that sort of thing these days. More

interested in fashions and film stars. Where is the girl, anyway? Never here when she's wanted, always around when she isn't."

"She was helping with the sausage rolls earlier but I haven't seen her for a while."

Billy Smith was in disgrace. Banished from the Hall, he loitered on the rough ground used from time to time for parking cars, of which there were now several in the village. He kicked stones and jumped in puddles, spattering his new grey shorts with mud. He let down the tyres on Finch's bike and hid the pump behind the dustbins. He swung on the chain link fence and scrawled on the posts with a damp piece of chalk. Bored, he went to the telephone box on the pavement and pressed button B. He pocketed two pennies and went down the path that ran along the far side of the Hall.

The privet hedge that separated the land from the field next door was ragged and overgrown and strayed across the path. But Billy was used to that. He had been here before. He pushed his way through the wet hedge and stopped outside the window of the dressing room. The glass was three-quarters obscured to keep out prying eyes. Billy was not disheartened. With a practised hand that belied his eleven years, he rolled out a beer keg from under the hedge, tipped it on end and climbed on top of it.

The dressing room looked empty at first. There was no light on but the sky was beginning to brighten now that the rain had stopped. As his eyes adjusted, he made out two figures writhing noiselessly on the lino. What were they doing? Was it a fight? Or a game? He tried to see more. Straining on tip-toe he lost his balance. As he tried to regain it, his hand struck the window with a thud. The sound made the man look round. Billy recognised him instantly. The man recognised him too.

"Miles, have you seen my badger?" said Lady Pamela Brockley. She was sitting at her dressing table in Brockley House, a short distance from the village. "I was going to wear it when I presented the prizes this afternoon."

"Any particular badger?" said Sir Miles, lying on the bed reading *The Times*. He radiated unconcern.

"The silver badger brooch your mother gave me years ago."

Miles sat bolt upright. "Oh, Lord. Not recently, no. Are you sure you haven't left it pinned to something? Have you tried your wardrobe?"

"I've looked everywhere. It's simply vanished."

"Surely someone has seen it. Have you asked Mrs Finch?"

"She disclaimed all knowledge of it. She was cleaning in here the other day, though."

"You don't think she...?"

"Who knows? I've no proof. She's always seemed pretty reliable."

"What about May? She comes with her mother sometimes. I remember her admiring it."

"Mrs Finch says May knows nothing either. And Max is a complete blank too."

"He always is."

"That's unfair."

"Could Prodgers have taken it?"

"I've worn it since he left."

"Well, it must be somewhere. It's bound to turn up eventually. Things always do."

It was some hours after the last event, the egg and spoon race won by Neville Filbert, that they found Billy Smith. He was under the bridge on the road to Easthampton. His neck had been broken.

Part Two

The Present

1

Jessica took the taxi from Nettlesham station to the Market Place. It was not far and, on any other day, she would have walked. She felt curiously detached, light-headed, as she was propelled through the narrow streets, the eclectic mix of building styles charting the history of the town. It was almost as if she were seeing them for the first time.

She was early. At The Copper Kettle she picked at a smoked mackerel salad she did not want and sipped a glass of mineral water, anxious to make it last. It would not do to drink too much. The heat was stifling and her oddly formal dress was attracting stares from children at a nearby table. She felt guilty she was not helping but she had been assured that everything was under control. "And we know how busy you are. We'll see you there."

The parish church of St Edmund's, Nettlesham, in the

county of Suffolk, dominated the Market Place and the surrounding town. Its well-proportioned tower of flint and stone rose high against the pale grey sky, high above the red tiled roofs, scarred by lichen and softened by moss, high above the blue-green cedars of the churchyard, weather-worn tombstones jutting through close-cut grass. The fifteenth-century church, with its fine tracery, unusual font and well-rubbed brasses of local worthies, was firmly on the tourist trail. Today, however, its doors were closed at two o'clock to all but those attending the funeral service being held in memory of Alice Mary Finch, known as May. Jessica crossed the Market Place some ten minutes before and took the place her mother was keeping for her in a pitch pine pew at the front.

May had lived in Nettlesham for over half a century. There she raised her daughter, Margaret Rose, and took a variety of modest jobs until her retirement some ten years before she died. Jessica, her granddaughter, had been at her bedside. May's aunt, Mabel Pargeter, with whom she had lived in the early days, had died only a year or two previously at the age of ninety-five.

The service was conducted with unexpected good humour by the Reverend Bob Goodboy, recently arrived from a parish in south London and already causing a stir with his banjo and bright yellow moped. Afterwards, there was a private committal at Nettlesham crematorium, a few minutes from the church by car. Among the many flowers, taken later to the local hospital, was a wreath of white lilies. A small card, edged in black, simply said, "In Loving Memory". There was no name, no mark, no indication at all of who had sent it.

Tea and sandwiches followed at May's former home, number twelve Oyster Lane. It was a small white cottage, bought and refurbished with her daughter's help. Among the many spilling out onto the lawn at the side this warm June afternoon were a number of men whom May had known over the years. They came to express their sympathy and good wishes but not to claim paternity of Margaret Rose. This remained a mystery. There had been whispering, of course, in shop queues and over garden fences but the gossip and tittle-tattle had faded away over the years. Now no one in Nettlesham remembered or cared.

Mrs Shepherd from number ten oversaw the refreshments, leaving Jessica and her mother, Margaret Rose, free to circulate as best they could. Her mother loathed the name, said it made her sound like a hairdresser or florist. She had dropped the Rose a long time ago. Now, plain Margaret Tate was a successful businesswoman in her fifties living in nearby Woodbury, with a string of adult shops in towns around the county trading under the name of Naughty But Nice. Penetration of Essex and Norfolk was said to be on the cards. Margaret's husband, Jack Tate, had fingers in a number of pies in the world of property development. A last-minute meeting with clients in Ipswich apparently kept him from attending today.

Gradually, the cottage began to empty. Fleeting glances at May's collection of bobbins, needle cases and pin cushions in the cabinet near the fireplace, ritual embraces, promises to keep in touch that would not be kept. Mrs Shepherd started to clear away the tea things with help from Mrs Lavenham from number fourteen. Uneaten sandwiches, relieved of their flaccid garnish, were grouped together on a solitary silver salver and offered round to the remaining few.

With a cheese and pickle in one hand and an egg and cress in the other, Jessica paced, wondering how much longer she would know this place. Sooner or later it would have to be sold. The sun came out and struck the bottles in the front window, bringing them to life, throwing lines of colour, blue and green, onto the sill and the rough stone floor.

On the mantelpiece, a vase of dried flowers and a couple of jugs jostled some sea shells and photographs in gilt wood frames. Jessica recognised her younger self and her mother as a girl. And the wedding at St Edmund's: her parents, Jack and Margaret. They looked almost happy. The wedding May herself had never had.

"She was a good friend to me, your grandmother," said Mrs Shepherd, one hand in the pocket of the flowered apron she had donned to do the washing up. "We went all over the place together. The beach, the estuary. Picking things up. Stones, driftwood, bits of glass, those shells there. They used to call us 'Flotsam and Jetsam'. A dab hand with the medlar jelly. She used to make that. And quince paste. Nice with a bit of cheese. Didn't see so much of your mother. But we went into one of her shops once. In Balding, it was. We had a right laugh."

Margaret was still in the garden. She was talking business by the lupins with a man with a black moustache, a large gold ring and an unpleasantly knowing smile. Left to herself inside, Jessica crept up the wooden stairs, as quietly as they would allow. Flakes of whitewash from the walls were caught in cobweb beneath the banister rail. Through force of habit, she knocked softly on the door of May's bedroom before going in. The room looked the same but felt different, empty, strangely still.

She sat down slowly on the edge of her grandmother's bed. It yielded with a gentle sigh. She looked at the familiar prints on the wall above: *The Haywain*, a Turner sunset, St Francis mobbed on the outskirts of Assisi by birds of uncertain species and improbable colour. With her left hand she traced the octagons of the patchwork quilt, pink and grey and powder blue. Her feet rumpled the rag rug on the bare floorboards. Bending down to straighten it, she saw that the door of the bedside cabinet was slightly ajar. Guiltily, she inched it open, as if a gradual breach made it less of an intrusion, less of an invasion of privacy. Somehow, it still mattered.

Under a pile of knitting patterns and a large bag of sherbet lemons, there was a box. Just a dull green shoe box. She removed it carefully. On the lid two words were written in black ink in her grandmother's neat and well-formed hand: 'Postcards etc'.

The only postcard was one from Margaret, taking a holiday of sorts by herself in Senegal. Otherwise, it was entirely etc. An old Post Office savings book, service sheets for Margaret's wedding and Mabel's funeral, a dark-blue passport long expired, two books of Green Shield savings stamps, a programme from the London Palladium signed by Arthur Askey… . At the bottom of the box was a slim guide to a country house. Brockley. The name meant nothing to her.

Jessica flicked through it. She found inside, slipped between the pages, a yellowed newspaper cutting, tightly folded in quarters, and a small black-and-white photograph of a young man in flannels and a striped blazer. She did not recognise him. He was not bad looking, in an old-fashioned sort of way, but there was something about his expression, his eyes, his sneer of cold command… . She frowned and turned the photograph over to avoid the penetrating stare, to see if there was a name. There was nothing.

She put everything back in the box and returned it to the cabinet. Everything except the guidebook and its enclosures. These she kept. They seemed to matter. She went quickly downstairs and put them in her bag, lodged for safe-keeping in the cupboard with the central heating boiler.

She joined her mother in the garden. She looked pale, delicate, standing next to Margaret, more finely featured. The Reverend Goodboy, fondling the ovate leaves of a Ribston Pippin, gazed at mother and daughter and shared a benevolent smile. A large black car came down Oyster Lane. It slowed almost to a halt in front of number twelve. The driver turned to look towards the garden but carried on without stopping.

2

It was not quite dark when Jessica got back to her top-floor flat in a large Victorian house in east London. Warm yellow light seeped between the drawn curtains of the basement flat. As she clicked up the stone steps to the front door she saw the curtains part tentatively. She made out the frail and faded form of Sylvia Beech, who kept silent watch on comings and goings at all hours of the day and night. Sylvia had little else to do.

Jessica picked up the box of organic vegetables deposited on the top step. Once inside the hall she placed it on the cold terrazzo floor by the door of the two Nigels, relatively recent arrivals to the house and known to Sylvia as 'The Boys'. Jessica had not been through that door in their time, had not entered the ground-floor flat since Alistair left last year. She wondered what he was doing now, who he was with. It had not been serious but it had been fun while it lasted. There had been no one since.

Upstairs, in her own flat, she exchanged her funereal black for something more cheerful and rummaged in the fridge. She stood at the kitchen window with a slice of quiche and looked towards the shadows of the park opposite. She would miss May. Uncomplicated and uncomplaining. Things can't have been easy for an unmarried mother back then. May had always been kind to her, close, understanding, complicitous. More like an elder sister than a grandmother, despite her years. Someone for her to talk to. Jessica, an only child, like her mother and grandmother before her.

She and May had both viewed Margaret with wry amusement and no great warmth. Margaret Tate, brisk and efficient, East Anglian Businesswoman of the Year, always just a bit too busy to pay her daughter full attention. And Jack — Jack The Lad, they called him — hovering in the background, sometimes there, more often not. What a pair, thought Jessica. Naughty But Nice? It was hard to imagine.

She took an apple from the bowl on the work surface, rubbed it half-heartedly on her dark red tee-shirt and went through to the other room. It was neat and tidy and bleakly functional. She always meant to do something about it, to make it more comfortable, welcoming, less like a base and more like home. There never seemed to be time. She worked too hard, she knew, spent too long in the office. But what else was there, just at the moment? Already, in her mid-twenties, she had a sense of life slipping away.

She felt tired from the journey and churned up by

the events of the day. But she did not want to go to bed and there was nothing worth watching on television. She put it on anyway, with the volume low, to break the silence, to introduce the sound of human voices, contained and controlled, without having to pay attention or try too hard.

Delving into her capacious black bag for a tissue, she came across the guide to Brockley House. She extracted it and settled down in the chair she had lugged back by herself from Only Collect, the junk shop in the High Road. The apple balanced, uneaten, on one arm.

The guide felt thin and insubstantial, as if it would fall apart at the merest touch. It proved more robust as Jessica read through it, pausing to glance at murky reproductions of prints of Brockley House in years gone by and of some of the treasures it contained. Or had in 1960 when the guide was published by the Heritage Commission. The author was apparently Lady Pamela Brockley, whose home the House had been. Here and there words were ringed or underlined in dark blue crayon, neatly but firmly, so that the impression could be seen on the other side of the page. Why these words had been selected in preference to others was unclear.

Jessica closed the guide and looked at the photograph and the cutting that had been inside it. She wondered why they were there. Had May just slipped them in at random for safekeeping or was there some connection between them? Where was Brockley, anyway? The guide assumed that people already knew. She went to the study that doubled as a spare bedroom. A sofa bed was her one concession to overnight visitors. The few who had slept in it, or had tried to do so, said it was the most uncomfortable bed they had ever encountered.

Sitting at the desk in the corner, she found the website of the Commission for the Built Heritage and Historic Landscapes in England, otherwise known as the Heritage Commission. She entered the word 'Brockley' and pressed search. Bingo! Brockley House, Brockley, near Easthampton, Hampshire. Eighteenth-century house and grounds...unique collaboration between Adam and Pratt...noted for its fine collection of Dutch and Flemish paintings...Bruegel, de Hooch, Ruisdael, Hals, Vermeer, Teniers... blah, blah, blah...Here we are. House open from 2 p.m. to 5.30 p.m. on Tuesday, Wednesday, Thursday and Sunday. At this time of year, anyway. Restaurant from 11 a.m. to 5 p.m., shop from 12.30 p.m. to 5 p.m., grounds from 10.30 a.m. to 6 p.m. Nearest station: Brockley 1 mile. Admission prices: bloody hell.

3

The Brockley page had a link to the website of the Easthampton and District Local History Society. Scrolling through it, Jessica found an extract from the previously unpublished memoirs of a visitor to Brockley House in the mid-1950s. It was too long to read on screen so she printed it out, curled up on the sofa bed and started to read:

> *Brockley House rose squarely from a gentle fold in the hills, surrounded by parkland that blended seamlessly into the countryside beyond. The House was built in the early 1760s a little way from the Tudor building demolished by Sir Matthew Brockley MP in favour of an improved residence, one that reflected both his ambition to be seen as a man of refined taste and sensibility and the favourable marriage settlement that enabled him to achieve it. And yet the House glimpsed from the drive through*

clumps of chestnut, beech and oak was at first sight a relatively modest affair. A simple expression of classical rules of symmetry and proportion, culled from the copybook by the architect Denzil Pratt, Brockley House was saved from austerity and chilly conformism by the warm red brick from which it was constructed. In the interests of economy, many of the bricks were recycled from the Tudor house.

Happily, Pratt was engaged by Sir Matthew to design only the outside of his new residence. For the interior, he turned to Robert Adam, whom he had met in Italy in 1757 while accumulating books, pictures, prints and sundry lumps of antiquity. For these, Adam created a house both elegant and sumptuous, celebrated far and wide for the quality of the fireplaces and the plasterwork of the ceilings. The more observant visitors may have spotted the recurrence of badgers worked unobtrusively into the design at the express request of Sir Matthew. If Adam had thoughts about the place of badgers in his conception of Brockley House he kept them to himself – or at any rate from Sir Matthew, whose family had long before adopted the animal as a whimsical device in the Brockley coat of arms.

In the intervening two hundred years or so the Brockleys served the community conscientiously, if without great distinction, and won respect and affection from their tenants and servants alike. Successive generations of Brockleys had, until 1935, represented the local constituency of Easthampton. But the historian who searches Hansard *for a record of their oratory in the House of Commons searches in vain. There is none. Loquacious in the Chamber the Brockleys were not, preferring to save themselves for the corridors, bars and tea rooms, lobbying quietly but effectively on their constituents' behalf. This gentle tradition of low-key Parliamentary service continued until Sir Miles Brockley, the tenth Baronet and present incumbent of Brockley House, decided, on the death of his father, to devote his energies to local government instead. As Chairman first of the County Council and then of the County Agricultural Executive Committee, set up during the Second World War to increase food production, he could scarcely resist the billeting of troops in the House when the time came. Indeed, Sir Miles willingly offered up his home to the greater good and retreated with Lady Pamela Brockley and their two young sons, Marcus and Max, to a small house on the estate known as The Sett.*

Brockley House suffered a good deal less than other properties requisitioned during the war. Ten years on, the scars of Nissen huts on the lawns had healed, the broken windows long repaired, the heads of decapitated statues retrieved and back in place, and the moustache scrawled on Gainsborough's portrait of Sir Matthew's lovely wife carefully removed. If the odd Chippendale dining chair had been chopped up for firewood by an errant trooper this was not a matter of great concern. There were plenty of others skulking under dust sheets in one of the servants' bedrooms on the top floor. They had been stored there by Sir Miles with various other items when the family returned to the House.

The Dining Room itself, tattered red curtains permanently drawn, was empty but for the heavy mahogany dining table that had survived the battering of ping pong balls and was now pushed hard against the wall. The Brockleys had retreated principally to the Morning Room in which plain utility furniture vied with the occasional reminder of an age of elegance and Horace, the Brockleys' golden retriever, aged and incontinent, relieved himself periodically on the Axminster. Meals were taken in the Kitchen downstairs.

Of the twelve servants working at the House in 1939 all had left to do their bit and not one had returned when hostilities ceased, preferring to pursue other lives in the brave new world promised by Mr Attlee. So the Brockleys made do with the services of Lorca, a Spaniard and general factotum, jack of all trades and master of none whatsoever. Mrs Collins came up from the village a couple of days a week to help with the cleaning while Filbert tended the

borders round the House when he was sufficiently
sober to do so...

*

Jessica woke up some time after two the following morning, cold and crumpled and stiff. She turned off the television in the other room, crawled into her own bed and went fast to sleep. She dreamt of badgers and men in wigs. As she got ready for work a few hours later her mind was only half on the meetings with clients during the day ahead. The idea of Brockley was beginning to get interesting and it made a change from work. House open Tuesday, Wednesday, Thursday and Sunday. There was no chance of going during the week, the way things were. It was difficult enough taking a day off for the funeral. Maybe the Sunday after next? At least it would avoid another weekend stuck in the flat.

4

The alarm went off at the usual time. Jessica lunged and silenced its piercing tone. She lay back in the centre of the bed and stared at the ceiling, wondering idly if the branching lines in the far corner were cracks or simply cobwebs. Edward, her well-worn bear of twenty-five years, companion and *confidant*, nestled beside her, gazing sightlessly at nothing in particular. One end of his ribbon, pale blue and frayed, trailed on her pillow.

The sun was shining this July morning, framing the edges of the curtains with brilliant light. Jessica's disposition was anything but sunny. She felt nervous, apprehensive, for no apparent reason. She wanted to shut out the day, to gather up Edward and curl into a ball under the quilt. But there was too much to do. She had a pile of papers to read before *The Archers* omnibus and then a train to catch.

At Waterloo, she found the Brockley train and installed

herself by a window. Her hand felt the rough smoothness of the fabric covering the seat. Her eye followed the intricate geometric pattern in ochre, russet and black, vaguely reminiscent of the 1930s. A shrill whistle sounded on the platform, the open doors beeped and glided to a close. Somewhere in the distance a coarse voice barked, "Stand away," not once but three times. The doors re-opened, closed again almost immediately and the train slid effortlessly out of the station.

She looked around the carriage. A man with wild hair and glasses, looking like the young Trotsky, had a large music score draped over his lap. He was conducting an invisible orchestra vigorously with a bread-stick baton. Two small girls with golden curls were sitting at a table on parents' laps, picking crayons from a box that had previously held mint chocolate chip ice cream. They were colouring outlines of circus clowns with great concentration. Close by, a balding man in a grubby sports jacket sat smirking with a slim volume. Smile became chuckle became near hysteria as the ticket inspector reached him. The man fished out his ticket for examination and the *Highway Code* fell to the floor.

Behind Jessica the door from the next carriage hissed open. A man with a battered leather bag strode past her, breathing heavily as if he had been running. He sank out of view in a seat beyond. She removed a small bottle of water from her own bag and took a lengthy swig. Book and iPod followed in quick succession and she settled down. A pink and silver sandal dangled from her right foot.

The train raced on. Jessica drowsed. Urban gave way to suburban and finally to rural. The sun shone on fields of corn too early to harvest. Chestnut horses grazed nonchalantly in groups of two or three. Friesians lingered in the shade of elder and hawthorn. Suddenly, a disembodied voice informed passengers that Brockley would be the next station stop and invited those leaving the train to take care when doing so. The train slowed over a level crossing, past a large new supermarket built in the vernacular style on the site of the old goods yard, past a car park largely lacking its weekday complement of gleaming cars, into Brockley station where it came to a halt.

Jessica woke with a jolt and looked dazedly around her. She picked up her bag and leapt out of the train as the doors were about to close. The train sped off to Easthampton leaving her alone on the bare platform. No one left and no one came. The station seemed completely deserted. She looked for the exit. As she made her way out to the station forecourt through a gate at the side she heard a squeal of brakes and saw a car disappearing in a cloud of dust.

"That was the taxi," said a man emerging from a corrugated iron shed behind an unruly hedge. He was wiping his hands on an oily rag. "It may be back or it may not."

"How do I get to Brockley House?"

"Left at the end and keep going. You'll come to the entrance eventually. Pity you missed the taxi. That's where it was heading."

She walked briskly though the village, keeping as best she could to the shade of high walls and high hedges, punctuated at intervals by the front gardens of small brick cottages and the entrances of well-kept estates. She stopped briefly outside Le Blaireau, a French restaurant commended by several reputable guides according to the stickers on the glass door. A small plaque to the left of the entrance said that the historic half-timbered building had once been the village pub, the Leg of Mutton and Cauliflower.

A little further on, past the village school and St Giles' church, she came to a large sign announcing BROCKLEY HOUSE in gold letters on a purple background. These were the colours of the Heritage Commission to whose care the House and grounds were now entrusted.

Jessica stepped inside a pavilion of faintly oriental appearance situated opposite the car park. She paid the entrance fee and bought a glossy guide. It was a lot smarter than the version she had in her bag. A lot more expensive too. On the cover of the guide was a reproduction of a watercolour painted by 'A Lady' in about 1825. It showed a prospect of the House from an unspecified part of the grounds. In the middle distance a couple strolled while sheep grazed peacefully around them.

"Can I interest you in membership of the Commission?"

inquired an enthusiastic female voice from behind a table piled with leaflets. "We refund your entrance fee if you join today."

Jessica declined politely and proceeded down an avenue of limes. A pale green light filtered through the sticky leaves. Two rabbits turned tail as she emerged into the sunshine at the other end. And there it was: a plain building in soft red brick, the east front relieved by a triangular pediment and pairs of fluted pilasters on either side of the entrance. She stood in the sun looking at the House, taking in its pleasing clean lines and simple proportions. The grainy photographs and second-hand accounts were beginning to come to life.

She went on past the House to the Tea Room in the Stable Block on the other side. A large poster pinned to a sturdy signboard advertised forthcoming events. Next on the agenda, she saw, was the Edwardian Weekend and Steam Rally in the meadows down by the River Brock. Lots of fun for all the family!

Jessica took her tray carefully over the uneven herringbone floor of the Tea Room to a table nestling in one of the original stalls of pale cream matchboard. A large hay feeder was fixed to the wall behind her. She forced her way into a pack of dolphin-friendly tuna sandwiches and looked at the guidebook as she munched.

The House, she learned, was given to the Commission by Sir Miles Brockley with an endowment provided by a relative of his wife, Lady Pamela, herself the eldest daughter of the Ninth Earl of Speedwell. The Brockleys transferred to a house on the estate where they lived until Sir Miles' death in 1980. Lady Pamela then moved into an apartment in the main house for the remaining ten years of her life. The present Baronet, the eleventh, was Sir Marcus Brockley, who lived with his family in the United States.

She poured a second cup of coffee from the cafetière, unwrapped her chocolate brownie and read on. A late eighteenth-century visitor to the House had described it as "commodious and convenient". After the Second World War most of the rooms were out of use and the House was anything but convenient. When the Commission took the property on, the priority was to carry out essential repairs, clean the House thoroughly and put things back in place. In the early years of opening to the public, Sir Miles and Lady Pamela themselves showed visitors around. It was not until the 1970s that the House was fully restored to what was thought to be its former glory.

The Commission had engaged the services of the interior decorator Meredith Faux, a partner in the well-known firm of Trompe and Faux. He had decided to adopt a scientific approach to the task through cleaning off the current whitewash and careful analysis of scrapes of paint. The resulting scheme was surprisingly colourful and later shown to be completely wrong. What Meredith Faux had painstakingly uncovered or reproduced was not the eighteenth-century arrangement but the redecoration of the 1880s. Whether that mattered in the least was the topic of occasional debate in scholarly circles.

Browsing through the rest of the guide as she drained her cup, Jessica stopped suddenly at the portrait of Lady Pamela in her early twenties by the artist Philip de Laszlo. She was struck by her elegant stance, her graceful Modigliani neck and her eyes, staring determinedly out of the canvas. Something about her rang a bell but she could not think why.

She made her way to the front of the House. A pair of neatly clipped laurels in square white planters stood to attention on either side of the steps leading to the entrance. Their formality contrasted oddly with the lavender lounging lazily across the path. Flocculent bees buzzed around it appreciatively on this warm Sunday afternoon. A flock of swifts wheeled high in the clear blue sky, squealing frantically.

Just inside the entrance, a man of military bearing greeted Jessica, checked her ticket and silently assessed the suitability of her shoes for walking on the floors and carpets of the House. The sandals passed muster. A small queue formed in front of her as bags declared by the bird-like woman behind the table to be too large or bulky to be taken into the House were handed over in exchange for purple tokens with gold numbers on them. She lingered over Jessica's bag, carefully considering its dimensions and the length of the strap. The bag was evidently on the borderline. She waved her through with an air of disappointment and pounced on the rucksack that was next in line.

In the Marble Hall, Jessica was assailed by a group

of children waving pencils and clipboards. They had been set the task of spotting badgers in various places in the House. Badger number one on the worksheet was somewhere in the Hall. She looked at Gainsborough's feathery portraits above the fireplaces. Sir Matthew and Lady Brockley seemed amused by the hunt taking place below them. Bowls of apricot carnations stood on the tables to right and left of the doors to the Saloon. The doors were open but the way was barred by a length of crimson rope sagging between two wooden posts. This was not the route the Commission wanted visitors to take.

As she was admiring the plasterwork on the ceiling the cry went up: badger! Not just one but several – lurking on the backs of the Hall chairs. She waited as the delighted children wrote on their worksheets and rushed off to repeat the task in the next room, ignoring pleas from the woman nominally in charge of them to WALK SLOWLY and NOT TO RUN. What *was* the collective noun for badgers? Herd? Troop? Pride? Crash? None of the above, thought Jessica. Time to move on.

She ambled through the Dining Room, in which a large mahogany table was set for a meal that would never be eaten. Cutlery and candlesticks gleamed coldly in the half-light permitted by the blinds drawn protectively over the windows. The plates and tureens on the table each bore a crest like the one on the back of the Hall chairs, as the children had no doubt detected.

"It's the original wallpaper." The words were fired from the woman sitting in the corner on a chair borrowed from the Tea Room. She wore a maroon trouser suit and clutched a plastic folder as if her life depended on it. "Hung in squares. There were no rolls before 1800." She stood up and Jessica moved off as a trio of fat men in Hawaiian shirts, shorts and baseball caps bounced into the room, talking loudly about the state of the nation.

In the Library, Jessica studied photographs on the desk, arranged around an elaborate inkwell and a large blotter. She was watched closely by a man with a large red nose and a small grey moustache. The man approached. The badge on the lapel of his blazer identified him as REGINALD TRUELOVE.

"That's Sir Miles and Lady Pamela on their wedding day in 1926, the year of the General Strike."

She saw a handsome couple framed by the doorway of a church, the train of the bride's silk dress flowing down the steps like spilt cream. Small children were throwing flowers at their feet. She nodded politely.

"This one's Sir Magnus with a shooting party in 1899. He's standing next to the Prince of Wales. Sir Magnus was Sir Miles' father."

Jessica ah-ed appreciatively at the fox fur and whiskers and guns at rest, broken over arms clad thickly in tweed and check.

"Over here we have Sir Miles' mother with the wife of the Italian Ambassador. And this is Lady Pamela in the uniform of the Women's Voluntary Service during the war. Ah, Lady Pamela. A fine-looking woman," said Mr Truelove distantly. "I knew her in her last years. She was very striking, even then." He looked at Jessica for a moment and said, "There are some more photographs on the piano in the Morning Room."

"That's a savage beast," said Jessica, to fill the silence. She was pointing at a polar bear rug dominating the carpet on the other side of the crimson cordon.

"It was found wrapped in polythene in an upstairs room. Put there during the 1970s' restoration, apparently. The tenant told us where the rug used to be. He knew the House as it was in the 1950s."

"In the eighteenth century plaster was based on lime, not gypsum as it was later. Lime plaster sets slowly so it can be worked by hand *in situ*." The woman in the maroon trouser suit had changed shifts and reappeared in the Red Drawing Room. The colours clashed horribly.

Jessica drifted apart from the group that had gathered to admire the ceiling. She found herself drawn to the Dutch and Flemish paintings, collected by Sir Matthew in the eighteenth century and kept together ever since, apart from a couple sold sometime after the Second World War. Big skies and churned-up roads, churches and watermills, markets and fairs. Skating and dancing, drinking and carousing, playing cards and making music. Glimpses of courtyards and ill-lit interiors. A girl with a parrot, another with a monkey. Tiled floors and carpets on tables. Buckets, bowls and flagons in abundance. Jessica's head was spinning as she carried on slowly in the direction of the Morning Room.

*

Twenty minutes later she was moving swiftly. She held her bag close against her. She felt guilty but exhilarated. It was pure impulse, done on the spur of the moment. She had seen her chance and taken it. Removing the bottle of water had created a bit more room. She had slipped it behind the chair vacated by the attendant, who had rushed next door to help his colleague restrain the badger-hunters hitting each other with their clipboards.

Her first instinct was to leave the House straightaway, to get clear as quickly as possible. But she had unfinished business. Pink and panting, she darted up the stone stairs between the Marble Hall and Dining Room. A large Gainsborough clung to the wall. It was his portrait of the Brockley sisters, Fanny and Lydia. One standing, the other sitting. Both with knowing looks and the ghost of a smile. As Jessica reached the landing outside the Chinese Bedroom, she hesitated, trying to decide which way to go. If she had turned round she might have seen the man with sandy hair consulting his guidebook at the bottom of the stairs. He had taken the taxi from the station and got to the House first, leaving his battered leather bag at the entrance.

She went into the Chinese Bedroom. A couple were inspecting the Kändler in the illuminated cabinets. She could see this was not right. She went back to the landing. There was a door marked PRIVATE, with a bell to one side above a chipped red fire extinguisher.

This looked more like it. She tried the handle. The door was locked. To the right the stairs continued. Not the stone stairs with the elaborate iron balustrade but a simpler wooden affair with plain white banisters. A NO ENTRY sign swung gently on a chain at the bottom. She took off her sandals, picked them up and was over.

Later in the afternoon Jessica was sitting on a large bench in the shade of a beech. The bench was said to have been made to the designs of Lutyens. Her eye followed the serpentine progress of a hose connected to a sprinkler some distance away. She looked at her postcards and at the mouse mat she had bought in the shop. The mat showed a badger, reproduced from the back of one of the chairs in the Marble Hall. She also took a furtive look at the other objects she had acquired. No one seemed to have noticed they were missing.

She did not usually take risks, do things without a clear plan, properly thought through. Spontaneity had always seemed faintly unwholesome, made her uncomfortable. And where would it lead? She needed to feel she was in control. Of course, she taken the guide from her grandmother's bedside cabinet on a whim but she told herself that was different, just salvaging a piece of her grandmother's past, obscure as it was, not really affecting anyone else. She got up and crossed the lawn, still feeling shaky, disconnected, invisible to the people milling around her. She was briefly distracted by a quincunx of mulberries planted over two hundred years ago, according to the guidebook. A small sign in purple and gold declared them to be specimens of the black mulberry, *Morus nigra*, and warned visitors to take care to avoid stains from the fruit. The Commission regretted that it could accept no liability.

She made her way round to the West Terrace. The sun was warm on her face. A mournful cry made her start. A lone peacock, blue-green iridescence against the rose-pink wall, was perched on a wrought iron table. She had read about the Gypsy's warning in the 1920s that the family would lose Brockley if the peacocks came to harm. Well, she thought, the family did lose Brockley in a way but the peacocks seemed alive and kicking.

She walked towards the Grotto and followed a path into the woods. The air was cool, the light green and gold. Beech mast crunched beneath her feet. A woodpecker drummed frantically somewhere close. She came across a small building whose pediment and pilasters mirrored the fearful symmetry of Brockley House itself. It was the old Ice House. She looked around her, took the bag off her shoulder and went inside.

5

Getting off the bus near Liverpool Street station next day, Jessica took her usual route to the office. People, buildings a blur as she thought yet again about the events of the previous afternoon. Tempered by cold reality and a sleepless night, exhilaration was giving way to mounting disquiet. What if she had been caught?

Clutching a Danish pastry from Luigi's on the way, she pushed the revolving door of Number One Pomona Court and entered the atrium. A man in blue overalls was on his knees, shining the leaves of plants sunk in a monstrous zinc container. She delivered good mornings to Comfort at reception and Dillon on security, swiped herself through to the lifts and went up to the fourth floor. The doors opened onto the dedicated reception area of Quarrenden and Cox, a region of thick pile, polished granite and soft lighting.

A wave in the direction of Leanne and Michelle behind the desk, another swipe through double doors, and she was in a long corridor recently hung with abstract works by the artist Lucy Potter. Senior Partner Arthur Turner, known throughout the firm as The Headmaster, was striding in the opposite direction. He looked a worried man. There were whispers yet again of merger. This time the smart money was on Paris-based Navet Bobigny, whose chief executive had been spotted in one of the corporate dining rooms only a few days previously.

Quarrenden and Cox were towards the top end of the mass of middle-ranking City solicitors outside the charmed group of firms known to insiders as the Magic Circle. Shortlisted for the last three years for Law Firm of the Year by *Wise Counsel* magazine, Quarrenden and Cox were growing steadily, opening offices in Brussels, Paris, Frankfurt, Madrid and New York. There were rumblings of discontent that new partnership opportunities had been largely confined to these locations. But this was of no immediate concern to Jessica Tate. She had only qualified a few months ago after challenging stints as a trainee in Litigation, Commercial, Environment, and Real Estate. She had come back to Q and C's Environment Department as an assistant in the small but productive team headed by Roger Pearmain.

She enjoyed the work and was told she did it well. She was highly motivated but not really committed. She never felt fully engaged; it was just a job. Her forensic skills and scrupulous attention to detail won admiration and respect from clients and colleagues alike. Yet there was something about her brisk professionalism and cool approach that made some people feel uneasy. She knew she should relax more, let the mask slip, learn to let go – if only she could see how.

Her fellow assistant, Clyde Pitmaston, dubbed her the Ice Maiden, said she must be frigid or repressed – but then he said that about many women who had the sense and discernment to reject his clumsy advances. Still, he had succeeded in prising her from the office once or twice to join the regular get-togethers of former trainees at Russets or one of the other wine bars in the vicinity. She was said to be a different person after a couple of large glasses of the house red but that always seemed to be after Clyde had left for his guitar lesson or salsa class or whatever else he was doing that night.

Jessica stepped over the piles of paper on the floor of the office she shared with Clyde, who was yet to arrive at eight o'clock this Monday morning. It was pleasingly quiet. She removed a brown envelope from her bag, put it in her desk drawer and headed for the kitchen. She took a short-cut through the café-style chairs and tables of the recently established break-out area, designed to encourage informality, relaxation and moments of quiet contemplation – when time permitted. It was part of Q and C's strategy for improving communication and promoting well-being among its staff.

In the kitchen she was assailed by notices about health and safety, first aid, promoting diversity, recycling bottles and cans, and the forthcoming quiz night. As she was about to pour the contents of her cafetière into her mug she was joined by Barbara Braeburn from Tax.

"I've just had a lecture on chargeable hours from the Rotweiller," said Barbara, blearily. "I'm falling behind on my targets. She said she'd been at her desk since seven and never did less than a fourteen-hour day. She'll be dead before she's forty."

"Roger's more concerned about his new beach hut at Southwold," said Jessica. "He's trying to think of a name for it. I suggested Mon Repos and Star of the East but he said they're too suburban."

She put her mug on the heavily ringed octagonal mat issued to all staff when Quarrenden and Cox achieved Investor in People status. She took the envelope from the drawer and slid two photographs onto her desk. Both were black-and-white and yellowing at the edges. The larger one showed a couple in front of a marble fireplace: Sir Miles and Lady Pamela Brockley, a little older but no less elegant than the couple in the wedding photograph she had seen in the Library the day before. Lady Pamela was holding a baby enveloped in a long lace christening robe. A small boy was tugging at his father's hand and trying to get away.

Jessica picked up the other photograph carefully. It was of two boys, one a few years older than the other, standing with a donkey in a field. The older boy had his hand on the donkey's nose; the younger stood a little to one side, both part and not part of the picture. On the back it simply said in pencil: "M & M, June

1943". She took a sip of coffee and looked at the younger boy again. There was no doubt about it. The passage of time could not disguise that look, those eyes. He was the same as the man in the photograph she had found inside the guidebook at her grandmother's.

A noise from the desk outside made her jump, brought her sharply back to the present. It was Linda, the secretary she shared with Clyde and Roger. She went quickly to the photocopying room, copied the two photographs she had secreted in a buff folder, and returned to her office. When Roger put his head round the door a few minutes later, he saw his assistant absorbed in a pile of papers about a waste disposal site proposed in the Green Belt.

"We've settled on Aqua Marina. Thought you'd like to know."

"Excellent choice," said Jessica, brushing some flakes of Danish pastry off the trousers of her charcoal suit.

6

It was already getting dark when she left Pomona Court that evening, once she had found a security guard to let her out. Probably the others would have left Russets by now. She had only said she would try to get there, told them not to wait. She was not in the mood anyway. She headed in the other direction, retracing her steps along familiar pavements. This morning they had been seething, now they were almost deserted. Laughter from an alleyway turned her head as a clutch of drinkers spilled from a pub. They looked relaxed and cheerful.

Back in her flat, she finished the take-away sushi from Anaguma, the new Japanese restaurant by the bus stop in the High Road, and looked around for *Bleak House*. She found it behind a cushion, a pre-war Everyman edition with a faded red cover that she had bought from a market stall one Saturday afternoon because everyone else seemed to have read it. She sat and stared at the book without opening it. It was not what she needed.

There was a pile of Georgette Heyers on the floor by her bedside cabinet, each with two words on the flyleaf: May Finch.

As Jessica drew the curtains in her bedroom, she glanced at the dusty black box next to the mirror on her chest of drawers. It was an unremarkable box, at first sight, with a simple brass keyhole and four squat little legs. The key had long ago been lost or mislaid. She saw the box every day but rarely noticed it. It was almost invisible, in the way of familiar objects, of things taken for granted. Tonight, however, she picked it up and took it to the bed.

She wiped the dust off the top of the box with a tee-shirt that was waiting to be washed. It shone bleakly in the harsh overhead light. The lacquer lid was inlaid with an oriental scene in mother of pearl. A many-tiered pagoda rose above misshapen trees bent by the force of an unfelt wind. Two stooping men crossed a gently curving bridge, like renegades from an early willow-pattern plate. She lifted the lid to reveal its mirrored underside and the velvet-lined interior of the box. As she did so, a tune started up. It was tinny and discordant.

She sat down on the end of the bed and let the musical box play on. It had just the one tune, plangent and melancholy. She never had known what it was. Neither had her grandmother, who had given her the box on her tenth birthday. Her parents had called the tune depressing but it had had a mournful appeal for the young Jessica. She had played it over and over again and filled the box with oddments – a plastic ring from a cracker, a butterfly hairclip, a lipstick smuggled from the girl next door.

Poor May. She died as she had lived, quietly and without fuss. The end, when it came, was mercifully quick. At least she was spared a lingering decline, the gradual erosion of mobility, dignity and sense. She had simply smiled, closed her eyes and slipped away. And then the blue-grey light of the church, the hymns whose words Jessica could barely mouth, the curtains drawing to a close as the coffin moved slowly away to be consumed by fire.

As the memories came flooding back, so did the tears. She reached for Edward and lay curled up until long after the music had stopped.

7

It was late August. Jessica was lying in the park opposite her flat with the wadge that was the Sunday paper. The grass was dry and brown and prickly. A company of starlings busied themselves in a nearby tree with much noise and the occasional flash of a glossy back. Two comfortably built women in white passed by on their way to the bowling green, taking furtive licks at dripping ice lollies. A grey squirrel darted in front of them, eyed them quizzically, and headed off in the direction of the Mediterranean garden, an area of gravel and drought-resistant plants recently established as part of the borough's response to the challenges of global warming.

Jessica yanked and extracted the Review section. As she flicked through it to get the measure of the day's offerings, a modest headline caught her eye towards the bottom of an inside page: 'Brockley old masters come back home.'

The article reported that two Flemish paintings,

missing from Brockley House for over fifty years, had been acquired by the Heritage Commission after a successful appeal, thanks to the generosity of a donor who wished to remain anonymous. The paintings were thought to have been sold by the late Sir Miles Brockley to raise funds to keep the House afloat in the lean post-war years before the Commission took over the running of the property. Both works were by seventeenth-century artist David Teniers the Younger, part of an extensive collection of Dutch and Flemish paintings assembled in the late eighteenth century by Sir Miles' ancestor, Sir Matthew Brockley. *Winter Landscape near Antwerp* and *Interior of a Tavern* were said to be in exceptional condition. They were shortly to go on permanent display at Brockley.

In response to a question about the security of the paintings following a minor theft at the House a few weeks ago, a spokesperson for the Commission said that suitable arrangements were in place. She was confident that an appropriate balance had been struck between safeguarding the contents of the House and enabling the public to enjoy them.

The article reproduced the pictures in colour and revealed that they would be on display from the following weekend. The House would open specially on the Saturday when a small ceremony would be held to mark the paintings' return. Perhaps, thought Jessica, it would be an opportunity to make some further inquiries. Surely, somebody must know something that would shed light on May's connection with Brockley and the man with the staring eyes. If the photograph was important enough for May to keep for all those years it was reasonable to assume that he had been important to her too.

8

She got there just in time. The House Manager emerged from a door in the corner of the Marble Hall. She was with a serious-looking man of middle years, who turned out to be the Commission's Regional Director for Southern England, and a less serious-looking man with floppy hair. She introduced him later as Hugh Mullion, Director for Conservation from the Commission's Headquarters somewhere in the West End of London. The crimson rope on its two short posts had been temporarily removed to allow the party to proceed directly to the Saloon. They turned right into the Red Drawing Room. Thickset security guards with close-cropped hair and steel-blue uniforms were posted at both doors. They reminded Jessica of the burly bouncers, humourless and unsmiling, installed at the entrance of Moonshine, the nightclub in the High Road.

She worked her way to the front. The pictures were not as she had last seen them. They had been re-arranged to accommodate the returning Teniers. Opinion had apparently been divided between those who wanted to reproduce exactly the arrangement shown in a photograph of the Red Drawing Room taken in 1925 and those who thought that the homecoming canvases should be hung in prominent positions where they could actually be seen. The latter won the day.

There were appreciative murmurs as Hugh Mullion, standing to the left of *Interior of a Tavern*, contrasted the boisterous scene, raucous and full of life, with the order and restraint of the classical room now containing it. He compared the rough stools and earthenware jugs in the picture with the clean lines and symmetrical form of the furniture and porcelain around it. He wondered what the popularity of such lively and uninhibited pictures in eighteenth-century England told us about those who claimed to espouse principles of order, taste and refinement. Good point, thought Jessica. What's the answer?

Mr Mullion's remarks about ruffs and stomachers in *Winter Landscape near Antwerp* were all but drowned out by the uncontrollable sneezing of the diminutive Floridian doubled up on Jessica's right. The offending visitor, wearing sandals and a flowered shirt, was led out by his discomforted wife.

In the Marble Hall afterwards, a cheeky reporter from the *Easthampton Advertiser* asked how the pictures could be part of Our Heritage if they were Flemish. Mr Mullion gabbled about taking a broad view, of seeing works as part of the contents of great houses and historic collections assembled over the centuries.

"I mean," he said, "if everything had to go back to its country of origin, there wouldn't be much left. Where would it all end? Think of the Elgin Marbles."

"I was," said the reporter, slipping out of the front door.

Jessica drifted towards the Tea Room. Many others had had the same idea. The soup of the day had long been exhausted. Not a ploughman's lunch remained. The sandwiches were down to a ravaged prawn mayonnaise and a sweating cheese and tomato. She settled for some Darjeeling and a slice of Mrs Oliphant's hand-made traditional carrot cake and headed for the seating area. Weaving her way through the throng, tray held aloft, she located a small table in a corner slotted between stall and stable wall. The previous occupants had just departed, leaving a mound of debris behind them. She insinuated herself onto a chair and pulled the table towards her. A harassed waitress, pink as a sugar mouse, relieved her of the rubbish and thrust it into a plastic sack.

Jessica poured some tea from the scalding metal pot, added the milk, and set to work on the carrot cake. A sepia photograph on the wall showed a group of gardeners and estate workers standing in front of a gateway sometime in the early 1900s. Flat caps, waistcoats and large buckets were much in evidence. She was admiring the whiskers of a man wielding a large spade when she heard a voice.

"Do you mind if I join you? This place is choc-a-bloc."

She looked up. It was a pleasant-looking man in, what, his late thirties or early forties? She had a vague idea she had seen him somewhere before.

"Please do," she gulped.

He unloaded his tray and put it against the stable wall by his battered leather bag. As he sat down, he said, "I think I saw you last time I was here. A few weeks ago. I'm Duncan, by the way. Duncan Westwood."

"Hi. I'm Jessica…Tate." She coloured and had another piece of carrot cake.

"There was a fuss because something was stolen. Two photographs."

"Really?"

Duncan took a fork to a slice of pecan pie. "Oddly enough," he munched, "I found the frames when I wandered into the Ice House. They were silver. I nearly trod on them."

"How did you know they belonged to the photographs?"

"I remembered seeing them earlier on the piano in the Morning Room. They were quite distinctive. I can't think why anyone should take the photographs but leave the frames. I told them at the gate on my way out."

"I hope they were grateful." There was an edge to her voice. Why couldn't he shut up about the photographs?

"Not particularly. But the funny thing is that I saw the frames today on the piano. With the photographs back inside."

"How strange."

"The room steward said they were sent back a few days after they disappeared. Carefully wrapped and undamaged."

"Curiouser and curiouser."

"No note or anything. Just a London postmark. EC something, I think she said."

"All's well that ends well, anyway."

Jessica sipped her tea. Her eyes watered. It was still too hot. Duncan swallowed some coffee and continued his assault on the pecan pie. After a while he said, "Are you here for the pictures? I mean the Teniers that have just come back to Brockley?"

"More the House, really, though I was at the ceremony earlier."

"I got here too late. I couldn't get near the pictures afterwards. It was much quieter in the Morning Room. I'll have another go in a bit. I'm preparing for next term's History of Art module: 'Dutch and Flemish paintings of the sixteenth and seventeenth centuries'. Sounds grand, doesn't it? Brockley has one of the best collections around."

"You're a teacher?"

He nodded. "In London. The Richard Brinsley Sheridan School, no less."

"Not the famous 'School for Scandal'?"

"The very same. That's about all we're known for after that business on last term's geography field trip to Malham Tarn. Not my subject, luckily."

Jessica smiled. She began to relax.

"How about you?" he asked, chasing the remaining crumbs round the plate with his fork.

"Me? Oh, I'm a solicitor…in the City…environment, planning, that sort of thing."

"Sounds very high-powered. Do you get out and about?"

"I jump into taxis to see clients. Go to the occasional public inquiry. That's about it. One conference room looks much like another."

"Well, you made it to Brockley, anyway. You must like it to come back so soon."

"I do. It's just the right size."

"You know, when I was here before I saw you going up the stairs. Then you vanished into thin air."

"Were you following me?" She sounded coy and wished she didn't.

"Just behind you, going in the same direction. At least, I thought I was."

Jessica hesitated. "I was exploring."

"How does that make you vanish?"

She leaned closer. "I went on up the stairs. Past the NO ENTRY sign."

"Anything of interest?"

"Not really. Just bare corridors and locked rooms. I came out at the top of the staircase on the other side."

"Were you looking for anything in particular?" It didn't seem like an inquisition and she was happy to go along with it. There was a reassuring matter-of-factness about Duncan's manner that put her at her ease. Nice brown eyes too, kindly, caring. And it was good to talk to someone about something that was not work.

"I was trying to see if there was another way into the Yellow Room."

"The Yellow Room." He repeated the words slowly. "Sounds like a Fu Manchu novel. Sinister and full of menace. The scene of unimaginable horrors – or maybe just an opium den."

She looked blank.

"Sax Rohmer?" he offered. "Well, anyway, I don't remember seeing the Yellow Room on the plan of the House."

"That's the thing. It's not. Look." She opened her bag and took out two documents.

"This is the current guidebook." It was a thick glossy A4 production lavishly illustrated in colour. She pointed to the plan of the first floor of Brockley House. "All these rooms on the left-hand side are shaded. That means they're not open to the public. I tried the door at the top of the stone stairs but it was locked. Now look at this one." Jessica produced a thin booklet, a little less than A5 in size, with a handful of illustrations printed in black and white. "This is the guidebook published when the House first opened in 1960."

"'Price One Shilling'," said Duncan, looking at the plain green cover. "It's five pounds now."

"The plan shows the Yellow Room on the left. The words have been underlined. The route was through the door that is now locked, into the Yellow Room, then into the Chinese Bedroom. That's the one you go straight into today. I can't understand why they changed the route. That's what I'm trying to find out."

"It was probably for some very boring reason. Perhaps the ceiling fell in or there was dry rot. Why is it so important?"

Part Three

1956

1

Lady Pamela Brockley sat at her dressing table in the Chinese Bedroom gazing at a landscape of mountain, willow and bamboo. Birds that might have been pheasants strutted between rocks; others roosted among flowering branches. She was looking at the original hand-painted Chinese wallpaper put up in Sir Matthew's day. It had survived remarkably well, she thought, all things considered. Perhaps a little grubby and worn around the light switches and by the door to the Yellow Room.

When she first knew Brockley in the 'twenties the place was well ordered and ran like clockwork. Servants went about their business discreetly and efficiently – cleaning, polishing, tidying rooms, making beds. She never actually saw it happen. It just did. She remembered the house parties, lasting from Friday to Monday, the music, the dancing, the conversation. Miles' mother was a formidable hostess. Thank goodness she and Sir Magnus could not see the state the place was in now.

Pamela sighed gently and reached for her hair brush. Its silver back gleamed dully in the February gloom. She recalled the first time she had met Miles. It was at a ball in London, somewhere near Berkeley Square. She pulled the brush mechanically through her auburn hair. That's right: it was Lady Sheringham's: for her twin daughters, Pansy and Poppy. Plain girls.

A handsome six-footer he was in those days, with a small moustache and soft grey eyes. Dove-grey, she had confided to her diary later. She had just come out and he had just come down from Oxford. It was not long before they became a familiar couple in society. They called themselves the 'Down and Outs'. She smiled at the memory.

Even then, Miles had no ambition to do more than bury himself in local politics and take over the running of the estate 'when the time came'. Still, she had no regrets, not really. People were as they were; you could not change them. The Brockleys had fared better than many landed families but she did not share Miles' optimism about Marcus following in his footsteps. Something had to be done to secure the future of the estate.

On the dressing table a tight bunch of snowdrops peered over the rim of a silver lustre jug. The smooth surface of the jug reflected the necklaces lying there, one of jet, the other coral. Pamela sighed and chose the jet, black against grey cashmere, as closer to her mood. She stood up and went slowly to the door of the Yellow Room, the room Marcus used to share with Max.

She opened the door and went in. The room was dingy and smelt musty and unused. She drew the curtains back with a jerk. The walls assumed a sickly, unhealthy yellow in the cold morning light of winter. It took the warm sun of a summer afternoon to transform the room into the bright golden yellow she remembered.

She ran her fingers slowly over the shallow depressions in the wall, just to the left of the photographs of rowing eights and coxless fours. Probably no one else would have noticed those gentle hollows, if they had not known. But she had been there, had seen the fist-shaped dents, the jagged edges, that night before Helga left for good, driven to the airport in stony silence by Prodgers, as it had been in those days 'BL' – Before Lorca. Two weeks later she had a letter from Helga's mother in Graz. The allegations were absurd. Max was only trying to teach Helga English. That was why she was at Brockley, after all. The girl was obviously highly strung.

Still, Prodgers had repaired the damage to the wall quickly and could be relied upon to be discreet. The remains of the chair went into the loft. The cushions she had mended herself.

Pamela straightened the pile of Hentys on the top of the chest of drawers and looked at the spines. *Gallant Deeds* and *No Surrender!, St George For England* and *The Dash For Khartoum, With Buller in Natal* and *The Bravest of the Brave.* Manly heroes and plucky chaps who played the game and did their duty for Queen and Country. It was a different world now. She thought again of her two sons, Marcus in London and Max abroad. She dwelt on Max. He had been away for over two years. She traced his name with a finger in the dust on the mirror. Why didn't he write more often? He knew the drill.

2

Has Lorca put a bucket under the skylight by the Nursery?" asked Pamela, as she closed the large panelled door of the Morning Room with her slim tweed behind. Pellets of rain drummed against the windows. She kicked into place the frayed velvet sausage that did duty as a draught excluder, held the tray hard against her and passed Miles a steaming cup of tea. Sitting up in his winged armchair, he removed the malted milk biscuit balanced precariously on the rim of the saucer, and broke it in two. His fingers were red with cold. He ate one half of the biscuit himself and tossed the other in the general direction of Horace. The Brockleys' golden retriever lay sprawled in front of the empty fireplace, apparently admiring the quality of the carving.

"Two," Miles replied. "He alternates the buckets at half-hourly intervals, when he remembers, and tips the contents down the Nursery basin."

"Perhaps he could mend the leak when the rain stops.

There's bright green moss growing on the inside of the skylight."

"I'll add it to the list of jobs," he said wearily. "I sometimes wonder whether we run the House or it runs us. There's always something. Paget was droning on again about selling the fields by the station to those builder people who want to turn the village into a suburb of Easthampton. He knows my views."

Pamela took a sip of tea and shifted in the chair in which she had installed herself below de Laszlo's portrait of her younger self. She was instantly recognisable despite the passage of some thirty years – and the headscarf and three jumpers she wore that wan March morning. Time had not extinguished the intensity of her stare or softened perceptibly the finely carved features that had earned her a reputation as a beauty in her day. The young Pamela stood cool and composed in her insubstantial white dress, the slender fingers of her right hand resting on the gilt back of a chair that had since succumbed to worm. The portrait had been painted in this very room, which faced east to catch the morning sun that seemed to shine every day before the war.

"Why employ Captain P as an agent if you won't take his advice?"

"He has his uses but he's no sense of history or the duties of a landowner. I have a responsibility for this place – not just to the present but to the past and to the future too. This is a family seat, home of the Brockleys for two hundred years. I'm trying to keep the estate together. I owe it to my forebears and to my successors."

"I know but…"

"Remember what Burke said?"

"No."

"'The ownership of land is a partnership not only between those who are living, but between those who are living, those who are dead, and those who are yet to be born.' My father taught me that and I've never forgotten it."

"This is the 1950s, Miles. Things have changed. Quoting Burke won't give us a new roof. Surely it makes sense to flog off a bit of land we can't even see from the House to stop it from falling about our ears. At the rate we're going there won't be a home to pass on to Marco, even assuming he wants to take it on. Talk about millstones."

"Marcus will come round. It's in his blood. He knows what's expected. He understands the importance of continuity. If Paget had his way we'd be submerged by a tide of mock Tudor villas. He even suggested cutting down trees in the park to sell the timber the other day."

Miles stood up gradually, putting his empty cup and saucer on the floor. A tall man, as old as the century but looking older, he was beginning to stoop, as if weighed down by the cares of keeping Brockley going. The air of quiet confidence and authority that had stood him in good stead in public life was increasingly tempered by an air of desperation. Living was more and more a question of survival. Horace staggered to his feet and lumbered with his master to a window looking towards the park.

The rain was beginning to relent. Droplets of water,

like distorting glass beads, clung to the upper part of the window frame.

"See those trees," said Miles, his breath condensing on the glass. He was pointing to the high clump of elms in which rooks were building their nests, as they had done every year he could remember. Pamela joined him and gently stroked his greying hair. "They were planted by Sir Matthew the year before he died. He knew he would never see the benefit. He took the long view. That's what it's about. Taking the long view."

"Letting the House fall down is hardly taking the long view. We've got to be practical, Miles. Why don't we open the place to the public, like Anne and Geoffrey over at Bedingfield?"

"And live in a goldfish bowl? Besides, the House isn't in a fit state to show to anyone, not even the great unwashed. Especially not them."

"Perhaps you'd better have another word with the Captain," said Pamela, straightening Miles' pink Leander tie. A sudden shaft of sunlight illuminated the daffodils on the baby grand that Max used to play. The flowers had hardly opened at all since she had put them there the day before.

A loud shriek brought Miles running from the Estate Office the following day. He saw Lorca, the Spanish butler-cum-everything else, attempting to herd peacocks with a pair of wooden tennis rackets he had found under the back stairs. The rackets were yellow and warped and varnish flaked off them.

"You bad birds," said Lorca. "You very bad birds. I put you in the Grotto."

The peacocks declined to co-operate and picked their way in various directions with studied indifference.

"Lorca. What on earth's going on? Leave the peacocks alone."

"They look at me with their tails. They give me the evil eye."

"Don't be ridiculous. You've seen them dozens of times before."

"They follow me. They want to get me. It is an omen."

"I hardly think so. Let me have the rackets. Now."

As Lorca handed them over reluctantly a peacock landed on the balustrade and looked at him with lofty disdain. A tail feather fluttered to the ground.

"Come inside and sit down."

Miles bent to retrieve an empty light ale bottle lurking between the leaves of some cream-coloured hellebores. The label had been half eaten by slugs. "Filbert," he said to himself. "Still, no chance of getting anyone else."

In the Stable Yard, *en route* to the Kitchen, Lorca stopped and said, "I forget. No, I remember. She was here."

"Who was here?"

"Señora Feench."

Miles frowned. "Mrs Finch was here? When?"

"One hour. Two hour. I don't know. She give me this for you."

Miles took the envelope that Lorca had removed from

the inside pocket of his maroon jacket, glanced at the writing and proceeded smartly to the House without another word.

"I've just heard it on the wireless," said Pamela as Miles burst into the Morning Room. "King Hussein has sacked Glubb from the Arab Legion."

"I expect that crook Nasser is behind it."

"I wonder what Anthony will do about it?"

"Not much, if recent performance is anything to go by. I don't think being PM is quite his *forte*. More to the point, what are we going to do about this?"

Miles gave Pamela the letter. It was a brief message written in thick black pencil.

"She can't want more, surely? We reached an agreement. This has got to stop."

3

Marcus Brockley woke with a start as the train drew into Nettlesham station on the branch line from the Suffolk town of Woodbury. He grabbed his canvas bag and scrambled out of the third-class carriage, slamming the door behind him. He made for a wooden bench on the platform as the chugging train drew out jerkily. His fine brown hair was sticking up at the back. A uniformed man in a peaked cap looked at him disdainfully, turned round and walked off.

Marcus removed a small notebook from his bag and reminded himself of the address of the house he wanted. He unfolded the hand-drawn map slipped inside the notebook, studied the route to his destination and set off towards the town, bag on shoulder and hands thrust firmly into the pockets of his beige duffel coat.

The path ran between the Woodbury road and the railway line for a while. On the other side of the line lay the estuary. The tide was out, exposing mudflats over which wading birds roamed and gulls flew low. Small boats lay stranded, helpless until the water made its return.

After five minutes or so Marcus crossed the road and made his way up Gravel Hill to the Market Place. A little way past St Edmund's church, he found New Lane. At the bottom, where the lane widened out, was a pair of thatched cottages painted a faded rose pink. A Hillman Minx was parked in front of them. Marcus opened his bag and brought out a camera. He looked round quickly and pointed it towards the cottages. A couple of clicks later he walked up the path of the cottage on the right, reciting his lines under his breath. He knocked on the door. There was no answer. He knocked again. This time the door of the left-hand cottage was flung open.

"What can I do for you, young man?" said a portly woman with white hair and a floral housecoat. The intervening fence offered no resistance. "You *are* young, aren't you? I can't see so well these days."

"Youngish, I suppose."

"Twenty? Twenty-five?"

"Twenty-six, as it happens. I'm looking for Mrs Pargeter. Do you know where she is?"

"Who's asking?"

"I am."

"Detective, are you?"

"Good Lord, no. Call me a friend of a friend."

"Well, she's not in. They all left half an hour ago." With that, the woman began to close the door. Then she paused and added through the crack, "They went to the fair: her, May and Margaret Rose. It's in the Big

Field on the other side of town. Back to the Market Place, down Sheep Hill and keep on going." She banged the door shut before Marcus could thank her.

Victor Maggs' Celebrated Steam Fair came to Nettlesham every year in May, turning the Big Field into a small shanty town of caravans, trucks, stalls and sideshows. Noise assailed Marcus on all sides as he penetrated the throng: the dull throbbing of the motors, the piercing screams of girls on the dodgems, the hectoring cries of showmen in bowler hats and elaborate waistcoats, all to the accompaniment of the *Blue Danube* waltz bashed out on the steam organ.

"Come along, come along. Loads o' fun for all the family."

"See the Nude Lady. Only a shilling. Nothing left to the imagination."

"Hoopla. Hoopla. A prize every time."

Marcus wove between the swing boats and the coconut shy, glanced at the Wild West Shooting Gallery and came to rest by the slot machines in the Monte Carlo Casino. His eye was caught by a machine inviting him to Test his Personality. The face of the machine was divided into segments like a giant grapefruit. Each segment bore the name of a trait or quality – domineering, naughty, flirtatious, cuddlesome... . Marcus put a penny in the slot, pressed the lever and watched the segments light up in turn, willing the light to stop at 'lovable', 'kissable' or even 'hot stuff'. It stopped at 'cautious'. Disappointed, Marcus moved on swiftly, wondering what had happened to Mrs Pargeter and the others.

He loitered by the roundabout, a heavily decorated baroque extravaganza adorned by dolphins and dragons. It began to move, faster and faster and faster. The garish gallopers leered at him maniacally. Up and down, round and round. Whirling, swirling, twisting, spinning. Everything became a blur. Marcus felt sick and giddy. He remembered that he had eaten nothing since a sausage roll the night before.

It was quieter by the caravans, resplendent in their livery of burgundy and gold. They were grouped in a circle around an oak tree, as if for protection against marauding redskins. A dog of indeterminate breed slumbered at the end of a chain outside a makeshift kennel. The door of the largest van opened.

"See you, Vic," said a woman with untidy blonde hair, dark at the roots. She straightened her skirt and clambered slowly down the steps. From his vantage point behind the tree, Marcus identified Mabel Pargeter. He had never seen her before but she was not so very different from the photograph creasing in his pocket. She was standing outside Brockley Village Hall with that man Stanley Finch, the caretaker, apparently unaware she was being captured on film.

Marcus followed at a distance. At the bottom of the helter-skelter she was joined by two others. May, he knew. He supposed she must be about twenty now. The small girl in the pushchair, obscured for a moment by a pink mass of candyfloss, could only be Margaret Rose.

He took a couple of pictures and turned heel. In his confusion he had completely forgotten his lines. Never mind. His journey had not been wasted.

A week later Marcus was in his room at the top of a house in Chelsea. He put another record on the record player – 'Frankie and Johnny' for the fourth time that evening – and finished the letter. He folded it, slipped two small photographs inside and inserted them into the envelope he had addressed. He propped it against the jar of peanut butter on the mantelpiece ready to take to the post office in the morning.

4

"I'm rather taking to this cooking business," said Pamela as they finished lamb chops, peas and boiled potatoes in the Kitchen at Brockley House. The rickety pine table bore the marks and stains of years. Thin cushions with Regency stripe covers relieved the hardness of the chairs. "Bit of a bore having to go and buy things, though. Mrs Snelgrove was telling me at the WI this morning that a new kind of shop has opened in Easthampton. Self-service, they call it."

"What's that?" said Miles, refilling their glasses with 1929 Médoc, the last bottle of claret in the cellar.

"Apparently, you wander around with a wire basket choosing the things you want directly from the shelves and pay for it all together at the end. You do everything yourself. No one has to serve you at all."

"Sounds like a sign of the times."

"Mrs Snelgrove doesn't like it. She says you can't chat to the shopkeeper or his assistant anymore without holding people up when you come to pay. They get very cross."

"Do they? They should be more patient. By the way, I got you that book you wanted at Heywood Hill's when I was up in Town. The Elizabeth David."

"*Summer Cooking?*"

"That's the one. I was flicking through it on the train on the way back. It has recipes for mulberry jam and jelly. It might be something we could do with our mulberries. Filbert was complaining that Neville keeps staining his clothes. I'm surprised he cares."

"I don't suppose he does. It's Mrs Filbert who does the washing – and practically everything else. She must have got at him."

"I bumped into the Thing of Beauty as I was coming out of the bookshop."

"How is Joy?"

"Vigorous, as ever. She accused me point blank of being cheerful."

"A monstrous calumny. What provoked this slur?"

"An unguarded smile, I fear. I had just overheard a redoubtable woman from the shires demanding six copies of 'Nancy's book on posh lingo' at the top of her voice. I can't think where I put our copy of *Noblesse Oblige*. Anyway, Joy said it was no time for levity at this dark moment in our nation's history, with our honour slighted by an Egyptian upstart and the mob howling at the door of No 10. She said Nasser was another Hitler and we couldn't let him get away with it. I thought she was going to provoke a riot in Curzon Street."

"She has a point," said Pamela, sitting up in her chair. "We can't just sit and do nothing. We should invade Egypt and teach Nasser a lesson."

"Rubbish," said Miles. "We should sort it out through the UN."

"The UN's just a talking shop."

"If we go in, we'll get the blame. They'll call us 'warmongering imperialists' and 'foreign aggressors'. Where will that get us?"

"Never mind about names. We need action, fast. The longer we dither, the worse it will be. Has no one learnt anything from appeasement?"

"Who in their right minds wants another war? It's barely ten years since the last one."

"But Nasser's holding the rest of the world to ransom."

"He's only nationalised a canal in his own country, for God's sake. It's just a change of management. He's hardly striving for world domination," said Miles, with a sudden flash of anger. He was dangerously pink in the face.

"Calm down, Miles."

"I'm not uncalm. If you ask me, the real problem is Dulles. He caused it all by pulling the rug on the Aswan Dam loan. I wouldn't trust him further than I could throw him."

"We can agree on that, anyway. Mrs Collins saw her son on the television at the No 10 thing holding a placard saying 'Peace Not War'."

"They have the television?" said Miles, dabbing at his brow with a crumpled silk handkerchief.

"Clubbed together and bought one three years ago for the Coronation. They haven't looked back. Apparently, they watch it with the curtains drawn even in broad daylight."

"I'd rather read a good book. Or talk to you, of course. Is Mrs C with her son on Suez?"

"I think she's more concerned about the brass. Keeps complaining about how long it takes to clean. I'm beginning to wonder whether we should have it lacquered."

"Expensive?"

"I don't know. It could be an investment. How did you get on with Mr Stoat at the bank?"

"He says he'll think about it and let me know. I'm not optimistic."

Pamela looked at Miles but only said, "I got some drawing pins for the wallpaper in the Saloon. Could you ask Lorca to stick it back."

"I'll add it to the list."

They finished the brie that Miles had bought at Paxton and Whitfield in Jermyn Street and drained their glasses.

"Why don't we have the rest of the bottle on the Terrace?" said Pamela. "It's a lovely evening."

"I'm always surprised by August," said Miles, leaning on the balustrade and looking at the setting sun. "It seems to start in summer and end in autumn."

He heard the yaffle of a woodpecker in the park, then nothing. He ran his hand slowly round the rim of an urn and felt the rough texture of the limestone, still warm from the day. A gentle breeze stirred Pamela's auburn hair, unchanged since Miles had first met her all those years before. He put an arm round her waist. For a long time they were silent, their faces illuminated by rays changing slowly from gold to salmon pink to magenta and then rapidly to darkness.

"Things don't seem so bad on a day like this," he said.

"I'm in the mood for Elinor Glyn," said Pamela.

"The tiger skin has been eaten by moth," said Miles. "I asked Lorca to put it in the attic."

"I'm not going up there. Would you prefer to err on some other fur?"

"There's always Oscar in the Library."

"Lead the way."

Afterwards, Miles lay with his head resting on the back of Oscar's, Pamela with her head on Miles' shoulder.

"Are you cold?" he asked.

"No, it's rather snug," she said, stroking Oscar's yellow-cream fur. "Lucky he was a big beast." Then she added, "I was thinking about Max. He's such a long way away. Do you think he's all right? We haven't heard from him for a while."

"We'd have heard if he weren't. Don't worry."

The light from the desk lamp was reflected in Oscar's glass eyes. They were clear and unblinking. The same could not be said of Lorca's as he unbent from the keyhole. "The Engleesh. They are crazy. On a polar bear with no clothes on. Is not like this in Andalucia."

5

At five in the afternoon a few days later, Miles was sitting on a bench on the Terrace attempting to complete *The Times* crossword. Horace was asleep at his feet, wheezing gently. A peacock was preening itself unselfconsciously a few yards away. Suddenly, the peace was shattered by the sound of children's voices.

"*Toro!*" they shouted in unison. "*Toro!* Where's the bull? We want the bull. We want the bull."

The sound was coming from the Stable Yard. Miles put his paper and pen down on the bench and went round to the side of the House. As he turned into the yard, he saw two small girls in gingham dresses jumping up and down on the cobbles. At the far end, their elder brother Neville emerged from a tack room and prepared to charge. Head down, with fingers for horns, he pawed the ground impatiently. Lorca stood in front of the girls. He removed from his head the battered Homburg he had found on a hook in the Kitchen corridor and tossed the hat into the air. It landed upside down on the ground. He saluted the girls and asked permission to perform and to kill the bull.

"Yes!" they shouted. "Kill the bull, kill the bull."

He turned to face Neville Filbert and sought to enrage him with the red tablecloth he now held in both hands. Neville charged. Lorca stepped deftly aside as Neville came through, head down. At each pass the girls cried, "*Olé!*" Finally, the moment of truth arrived. Lorca took a wooden spoon from his pocket and appeared to plunge it, handle first, between Neville's shoulder blades. Neville fell to the ground. In a strangled Bluebottle voice he said,

"I do not like this game, my Capitain. You have deaded me, you dirty rotten swine, you."

The girls showered Lorca with roses evidently taken from the bed below the Terrace. As he took his lap of honour he caught sight of Miles leaning against a pillar by the entrance to the yard.

"Oh, Sir Brockley," he stammered. "Is a bit of fun. Just a bit of fun. Neville not really dead. Get up, boy. Get up."

"Thinks," said Neville, still in Bluebottle mode. "I am not deaded after all. Goody, goody."

"That's a relief," said Miles, smiling broadly. "Why don't you have some lemon barley water. We may even be able to run to some biscuits."

Lorca took the Filbert siblings to the Kitchen. Miles retrieved his hat from where it had landed, brushed off most of the dirt and went back to the Terrace where Horace remained fast asleep.

*

At much the same time, Tom Filbert, the children's father, was in the Walled Garden. It was a pale shadow of its former self. Once it had provided fruit and vegetables for the household and flowers for the rooms. Now the glasshouses and cold frames were abandoned and the beds undug for years. Dandelions, nettles and couch grass thrived in place of potatoes, carrots and peas. Wasps feasted on fallen damsons and apples rotted on the trees. Filbert made his way to the woodpile by the far wall, cursing under his breath as brambles and bindweed conspired to impede his progress. When he reached the logs, silver-grey with age, he bent down and removed some carefully. He put his hand in the gap. It was quite dry. He felt around tentatively. His fingers touched something that felt both soft and hard.

"Still there," he muttered. "Let's leave it a bit longer."

He returned the logs to their places and went back the way he had come. He helped himself to some of the remaining Worcesters and pulled the garden door hard behind him, brushing the flakes of pale blue paint from his sleeve.

6

Miles limped into the Marble Hall, a pallid cube at the centre of the House adorned by carving and plasterwork that contrived to be both elaborate and restrained. He headed for a chair and bent down with a grunt to remove a stone from his shoe. On the back of the chair, as on the backs of the others placed in pairs round the walls, a painted badger looked uncertain above the Brockley family motto: *Ecce meles, ecce homo.* Behold the badger, behold the man.

Miles put the stone in his jacket pocket and pulled out a bill for work to houses on the estate. At least they were in a decent state of repair. He would find the money to pay the builder. His first duty, he reflected, was to his tenants. Even so. Even so.

He looked around him in the pale grey autumn light, the scene enlivened by chrysanthemums, burnt orange and rust, placed by Pamela on the tables either side of the doors to the Saloon. She said that flowers would cheer the place up a bit. Before the war, they used to put a Christmas tree from the estate in the middle of the Hall, narrowly avoiding the ceiling. Miles himself had dispensed punch to servants and tenants and given them their presents. It seemed like another age.

Above the empty fireplaces, on opposite walls, hung Gainsborough's relaxed portraits of Sir Matthew and Lady Brockley, superimposed on improbable wooded landscapes. Despite the benevolence of their gaze, Miles felt judged by them. He knew he had let them down.

The hard wooden chair on which he perched offered no encouragement to linger further. His footsteps echoed sharply on the marble floor as he headed for the Saloon where he had played football with Marcus and Max on rainy days. Opening the double doors, he proceeded smartly to the Red Drawing Room. Between pictures of drunken peasants and skaters on a frozen lake, members of Brockley's extensive collection of Dutch and Flemish paintings, two empty spaces stood like an accusation. Miles frowned. He had had no option, but never again.

The screech of brakes on gravel heralded the return of Lady Pamela. Lorca was at the wheel of the 1938 Humber Snipe. Miles went to the front door to meet her as Lorca took the car round to the stable that served as a garage.

Pamela came up the steps unsteadily and rested her hand on a pillar. She looked pale and drawn.

"What's the matter?" said Miles.

"My stomach's still at the station," she said, catching her breath. "I think Lorca's trying for a new land speed record. Fortunately, the driver of the Easthampton bus managed to pull off the road. The ditch was quite shallow. Next time I'll walk from the station."

"Come and have a drink." He led her to the Morning Room and dispensed manzanilla. "How was the great Metropolis?"

"It gets worse," she said, smoothing her dress of soft green silk. The colour was beginning to return to her cheeks. "The Underground was frightful. People everywhere. Talk about vile bodies. Such a pity you have to encounter so many people you don't want to meet in order to see the few you do."

"All right once you got to Chester Square?"

"An oasis of calm. Aunt Violet had the OM in tow. He's only after her money but she dotes on him. Heaven knows why. He's hardly one of us."

"The Ordinary Man is the future," said Miles. "We're a dying breed."

"He kept calling her 'Ducks'. She giggled like a schoolgirl. At her age. Not that she looks it."

"*She may very well pass for forty-three / In the dusk, with a light behind her,*" sang Miles.

"I expect she'll outlive us all."

"Any of the old gang?"

"Margot Lane. I haven't seen her for years. She and Ronnie are selling Dogwood to developers and moving to the south of France."

"Another one gone," said Miles. "I was at school with

Ronnie. We were in the same House. We used to call him 'Mincing Lane'. I was a bit surprised when he married Margot."

"Weren't we all. I gather they had an understanding. Rosy Hill came up and asked me if Marco was an Angry Young Man. I said he was a bit miffed when he dropped half a pound of butter on his new suede shoes. Rosy's daughter saw him at a bottle party in Chelsea the other night. Full of artists and musicians. Apparently, a fight broke out with some sailors and the police arrived. Marco slipped off in the nick of time with some girl, rumoured to be an art student."

"I wonder when we'll see him. There are things we need to discuss. I have a treat in store for you: vegetable soup and a cheese omelette. Not quite the Ivy but it'll keep the wolf from the door."

7

Marcus Brockley paused outside the unassuming frontage of the Venezia coffee bar, located next to a patisserie in Lemon Street, Soho. Using the glass door as a mirror, he ran a comb quickly through his hair and went in. It was narrow and cramped inside. He squeezed past the juke box and greeted the girl sitting patiently at the small square table with an empty coffee cup and a packet of Craven A. Her face was deathly pale, like a corpse, an effect heightened by the liberal use of mascara and her tight black jumper.

"Sorry I'm late, Stella," said Marcus, placing a kiss on her bright red lips and putting his duffel coat on the back of the chair. "I went back to the house to get changed. I have to wear a suit at the agency. I've spent all day trying to think up a slogan for fish fingers. My mind was a complete blank."

She looked thoughtful, but not for long. "How about: 'The taste of fresh fish without the fuss'?"

"Stella, you're a genius. Coffee?"

The gleaming Gaggia spluttered and hissed. Marcus returned with two transparent cups of dark brown liquid and a threepenny bit for the juke box.

"Mario wasn't best pleased about giving me this for twelve farthings."

"They're temperamental, these Italians. It's the Latin blood."

"Italian as haggis, if you ask me. Probably a refugee from the Glasgow ice cream wars. What's it to be?"

Too late. A brylcreemed youth had got there first.

"Not 'Rock Island Line' again," said Stella. "That's the third time since I've been here. Why are you wearing odd socks?"

"It's an unmatching pair," said Marcus, stretching out his sandalled feet to admire the effect. "One red and one yellow. Reminds me of the Pied Piper. I borrowed them from my father the last time I was down at Brockley. He had another pair just like them. At least, he does now."

"And when am I going to see the ancestral home? You keep putting me off."

"When the time is ripe. I warn you, it's magnificently uncomfortable. 'See Brockley and freeze in style.' I must remember that. Wait until there's a heat wave."

"Are you ashamed of me?"

"Of course not. I just feel the weight of expectation on me when I'm down there. Elder son and all that. Got to do my duty. I'm supposed to run the place 'when the time comes', as they put it. Not that it will come, the way things are going. We'll all be blown to smithereens before long."

"Cheerful today, aren't we?"

"Well, what's the point? How can anyone think about the future of a small country estate in southern England when the end of the world is just around the corner? Four minutes and then…"

"What?"

"Nothing. Nix. Oblivion. Even for Mr Adam's handiwork."

"It may never happen. Life carries on. It's not all bad. Every cloud has a silver thingy."

"Does that include a mushroom cloud?"

The coffee bar was filling up in anticipation of Keith Menace, until recently known as Terry Fish on the streets of Bow where he had been born and brought up. The leather-jacketed Menace was in a huddle in the far corner on the small raised platform that passed for a stage. Marcus caught a glimpse of a washboard and a tea chest bass with a broomstick handle.

A man with a beard pushed his way though the crowd. It was Howard Wheeler, a friend of Stella's. Like Marcus, he was wearing a polo neck jumper and corduroy trousers. Unlike Marcus, his clothes were stained and frayed. Stella slid onto Marcus' lap and offered Howard her chair.

"They've caught up with me," he said, sitting down with a heavy sigh. "I've had my letter. I'd hoped they'd abolish National Service before it was my turn. Perhaps I'll be shipped out to get shot in Egypt."

"Or Cyprus," put in Stella. "Our next door neighbour's son got killed there."

"Or you could live to tell the tale," said Marcus, encouragingly. "Most people do. I did."

"When was that?" said Howard, hand-rolling a cigarette with some difficulty.

"Before I went up to…university."

"Army?"

"Yes. I came out two inches taller. They won't let you keep that beard." Marcus had to shout above the mewling, whining, throbbing and scratching of Keith Menace and his Skiffle Kings.

"Fancy a jazz club?" said Howard later.

They fell out of the fug into the cold autumn air. A quarter of an hour later they fell down some steps into a basement somewhere off Piccadilly. The club was hot and crowded. It smelt of sweat, stale beer and cigarette smoke. Marcus forced his way to the bar and bought brown ales for Howard and himself and a Babycham for Stella. On stage, Pete Ebbisham's All Stars were in full swing. Known to their fans and fellow jazzmen as the Peas, the band drove around the country from date to date in a battered Volkswagen van affectionately called the Pod. Pete himself, three sheets to the wind, was teetering at the front with a trumpet. Only the lightning reaction of the clarinetist prevented him from going over the edge.

A roar of applause greeted the arrival of Delilah Samson, the band's female vocalist. She was dwarfed by the massive form of the double-bass player. Delilah swayed pleasingly in an emerald green dress, purring in a soft, mid-Atlantic accent that reverted off-stage to her native south London. She alternated with a stoutish man apparently intent on devouring the microphone. He affected a trilby and a loud striped blazer, unpleasantly stained under the armpits.

"Who's that?" said Stella between sets. She pointed to a tall man leaning against the bar. He was deep in conversation with a shorter one, who wore a black shirt and white tie. "He looks like a guardsman."

"I'm sorry, I haven't a clue," said Howard.

"I must get back," said Marcus. "Some of us have work to go to in the morning."

"Can I come too?" said Stella. "I can't face Mrs Nugget. 'No Blacks, no Irish and a shilling for a bath.' She's guaranteed to wake up the moment I open the front door."

They looked at Howard.

"I could go to the Lyons Corner House at Charing Cross," he said, doubtfully. "You can spend the night there for the price of a cup of tea – so long as you stay awake." He yawned loudly.

"All right," said Marcus. "Come on. But it will have to be the floor."

The three made their way from the bus stop in Chelsea to the stuccoed house of Henry and Joan Fawcett, friends of the Brockleys from the old days. Marcus had a room on the top floor. As they neared the house, Howard collided with a cluster of empty milk bottles and send them tumbling and spinning across the pavement.

"Quiet," said Marcus. "I'm not supposed to have anyone back at night."

Howard picked up a bottle, held it like a microphone in both hands and started to croon about his very good friend the milkman.

"Will you be quiet."

Howard giggled, put the bottle down with surprising delicacy and relieved himself in a large flower pot by the front door.

"The geraniums will soon be over," he said.

"They will now."

Marcus opened the front door gently and let them in. Apart from the hall, the house was in darkness. He found the switch to light the stairs and landings and the trio made their way with much shushing up to the top floor. Still wearing his duffle coat, Howard lay on the sheep skin rug in front of the gas fire and went fast to sleep. His breathing was heavy and uneven. When he began to snore Marcus kicked him and went to make some coffee.

Stella looked at the books and records that she had been in no state to notice when she came back after the party a few nights before. "Is this the one everyone's making a fuss about?" she said, removing a book with a torn yellow jacket from the pile on the floor.

"*The Outsider*? Yes. Pretty impressive, as the author

is the first to admit. A hard act to follow. And he's two years younger than me."

Stella stepped over the foetal form of Howard Wheeler to look at the frameless photograph curling on the mantelpiece next to a packet of fig rolls. It showed two boys standing in front of an elaborately carved fireplace.

"Is this you?" she said, pointing to the taller boy as Marcus put the coffee on a low table in front of the settee.

"Yes. Taken just after the war. We hadn't long been back in the big house. The place was a tip."

"So who's the other one?"

"That's Max. He's my younger brother."

"How much younger?"

"Three years."

"Hm. He looks…determined, doesn't he? As if nothing would stand in his way." And no one, she thought uneasily. "What's he like now?"

"I haven't seen him for a couple of years or so. I don't suppose you will either. He's out of the country. Now come and sit down – without treading on Howard."

8

Riots in Trafalgar Square, Russian tanks roll into Budapest and we're holding a coffee morning for the WI. What a life," said Miles, taking a cobweb brush to the pediment above the door from the Marble Hall to the Dining Room corridor.

"Coffee morning *and* bring and buy sale," corrected Pamela, her foot firmly on the bottom rung of the wooden step ladder.

"Oh, well, that makes all the difference. We'll despatch a few crocheted rabbits to the nearest Hungarian relief centre. Send a bunch of crocheted carrots to go with them."

"Don't let Mrs Tansy hear you. She's been at it with her hooks all year. Now, where is Lorca with those trestle tables? I want some here in the Hall for the coffee and cakes and the rest in the Saloon for the bring and buy. Come down from the ladder. I'm going to the Kitchen to see what Mrs Collins is up to. She's grumbling that serving coffee to the WI ladies is beyond the call of duty. I expect I'll end up having to do it myself."

"Mrs Finch never complained."

"No, well…that was then."

"Are we at war with Egypt over the Suez Canal?" asked Miss Cumber, nibbling tentatively at a rock cake in the Hall.

"They're calling it a state of armed conflict," said Mrs Norris, singeing gently by the single-bar electric fire. "I heard it in the haberdashers in Easthampton."

"No, no, no. It's 'Police action'," said Mr Norris authoritatively. "That's the term." He had only come to carry a box of hot water bottle covers but fell prey to a slice of Victoria sponge.

"It's madness, whatever you call it," boomed Miss Punnet. "An act of folly. It'll end in tears. Mark my words."

"I'm sure the Prime Minister is doing his best. Such a gentleman. And so well dressed."

"Over-dressed if you ask me. Never trust a man that wears a double-breasted waistcoat."

"He's a real charmer. And quite a ladies' man, I'm told."

"He's got the backbone of a jelly fish. They should bring back Churchill."

"Churchill's totally gaga. All he can manage is brandy and cigars."

"At least Britain was something in his day. We're hardly top dog now."

Horatio looked mournful and ambled into the Saloon.

"And we've let the Russians get away with it in Hungary."

"It's a humiliation."

"I think people are being very unfair. Have you seen the papers?"

"We don't take the *News Chronicle* in our house any more. Not after what it said."

"At least it has the guts to take a stand against this government."

"They should put a woman in charge."

"We've got a Queen. And very nice she is too."

"I mean as Prime Minister."

"A woman Prime Minister? It'll never happen," said Mr Norris confidently.

"Can I tempt you to a doily, Sir Miles?" beamed Mrs Quince.

"Actually, I was rather taken with your charming lavender bags. Would a brace be in order?"

"Oh, Sir Miles. How kind. I'll set them aside for you."

"What on earth are you going to do with those?" breathed Pamela.

"Well, charity begins at home and all that. Perhaps I'll give them to the Filbert girls."

"It would be better if we started to sell off some stuff ourselves. We've got to do something. Mrs Snelgrove was telling me about Hughie Green."

"Is he the new barman at the Leg of Mutton?"

"He's on the television. He's the host of a programme on the commercial channel they have now. It's called 'Double Your Money', or something like that. Sounds rather a good idea. Perhaps we should try it."

"Twice nothing is still nothing. Still, at least that means we've nothing to lose."

"'Remember, remember, the fifth of November'," chirped Mrs Firth. "Are you coming to the fireworks tonight, Sir Miles? Seven-thirty on the green. We rather hoped you'd do us the honour of lighting the bonfire again this year."

"We're looking forward to it."

"Splendid. The Colonel will be bringing some of his mulled wine."

"It wouldn't be the same without it."

In Brockley village that evening people were assembling in dribs and drabs on and around the green. A loose rope separated them ineffectively from the bonfire and the firework area beyond. Lorca stumbled through the thick grass, holding a paper cup. He had had little difficulty choosing between the mulled wine and the orange squash. He stopped suddenly. "What is that?" he said, pointing to the figure slumped in a wheelbarrow.

"That's the guy," said Pamela, giving a penny to a small boy in cub uniform. "He's stuffed. He'll be thrown on the bonfire and burnt. It's an English tradition."

"He is very smart. He wears a suit. And he has a

painted face with a moustache. It looks like your Prime Minister. I see him in the newspaper."

"Good God, you're right. It does look like Anthony. How funny. I wonder who did that?"

9

Miles removed the blue and white vase from the table in the Morning Room next day and put it in the fireplace. He pulled the table away from wall, turned it round and lifted the top to reveal the green baize beneath. He tucked the dangling end of his scarf into his coat and extracted a pack of cards from the drawer.

"I thought we were playing Bézique, not Piquet?" said Pamela, dragging a chair to the table. "We'll need another pack."

Miles grunted and scrabbled in the drawer to find one more set of cards with the same floral backs.

They took off their pigskin gloves, picked up a pack each and worked their way through, discarding all the cards of six and below, as the game required. Miles gathered these up, put them under his chair and shuffled the cards remaining on the table.

"You can deal," said Pamela. "It's about time we got that fire going."

"The chimney's still blocked. It's on the list but not at the top." Miles cut the cards, put them back together and dealt eight each. "Where's the electric fire we had in the Hall yesterday?"

"I said Lorca could take it to his room. It's even colder up there."

"What about the paraffin stove?"

"Still in the Kitchen corridor waiting for the paraffin."

"I'll get some at the shop. What's our limit? Two thousand?"

Pamela nodded and led with a seven of hearts.

"Paget says I should put the rent up but I'm not keen. It's just dumping the problem on the tenants. He's investigating the grant situation."

"We should have a major rummage upstairs. I mean it, Miles. There are doors I haven't seen behind for years."

"We might find more than we bargained for."

"I can cope with the odd pigeon."

"I meant something more serious. Like a ceiling down or dry rot. Sometimes I'd rather not know."

Miles played a ten of hearts and took the trick.

"Four Kings."

"Eighty," said Miles. "Paget says nothing will be the same again."

"What?"

"Suez. The ceasefire. He calls it 'the climb-down'. Says he's ashamed to be British."

"We should have seen it through, not given up half-way."

"We shouldn't have gone in at all – but you know my views."

"Yes," said Pamela, playing an Ace of Clubs.

"It's Anthony I feel sorry for. A sad end to a distinguished career. Now he'll be remembered for this ludicrous escapade."

"He hasn't gone yet."

"It's only a matter of time. Who do you think it will be? Harold or Rab?"

"Harold."

"I fear you may be right. Only one good thing can come out of this sorry saga."

"What's that?"

"That we learn never to get mixed up in the Middle East again without UN backing."

"My trick."

10

It was barely light when Filbert left Flint Cottage. He removed three bottles of beer from the wooden crate by the back door, and put them in his bag with the packet of ham sandwiches and hardboiled eggs provided by his wife. It had rained during the night, filling the ruts in the lane with water. He made his way along the lane following the high brick wall on his right. Wet leaves stuck to the soles of his boots. He rubbed his unshaven red face and thought: it won't do to leave it there in winter; best take it out and put it somewhere else.

"Good morning, Mr Filbert," said the Misses Thompson gaily as they rode through the puddles on identical black bicycles. "They say the forecast is good." He mumbled something and stopped in front of the gate in the wall that led into the grounds of Brockley House. He opened the gate without pausing to look up or down the lane. Had he done so he might have spotted the angular figure of his son Neville, part-time bull and general layabout, a little way behind him.

Filbert passed the Lake. Mist was rising from the surface. Mallards near the water's edge quacked gently about their business. His boots and trouser bottoms were sodden from the long, wet grass. He was unconcerned. His mind was on his mission. He wanted to get that over with before starting on the beds on the south side of the House.

In the Walled Garden he carefully removed the package from the woodpile and put it in his bag. He took out a bottle and forced the top off with a jolt against the sharp edge of a log. A little later he repeated the process. He burped and threw the empty bottles into the nettles. One bottle left. Better get to work.

A pink sliver of light softened the eastern sky as Filbert traipsed through the grounds. He took a short cut along the top of the ha-ha that separated the park from the formal gardens nearer the House. Three-quarters of the way along he slipped, lost his balance and fell with a dull, scarcely audible cry of surprise. He lay at the bottom of the ha-ha and did not move. The bag was on top of him, the strap off his shoulder and twisted over his arm. As he rounded the corner Neville heard the doleful sound of a peacock. His father had disappeared from view.

"We shouldn't have started in the attic," said Pamela, sneezing violently. Motes of dust rose thickly in the shafts of light penetrating the gloom through gaps in the roof. Her torch was beginning to fade.

"It would help to know what we're looking for," said Miles. "And we need some more buckets up here. You can see where the rain got in last night."

"There must be something – anything – we can sell for a bob or two."

"We've already looked in those trunks. That one's the stuff I had at St Luke's and that's my father's from the First War."

Pamela lurched towards a large gathering of tea chests: "One…two…three…fifteen tea chests. All empty, if you discount the dirt and the pigeon droppings."

Miles made his way to an iron bedstead by the water tanks. It was covered in old army blankets and shredded newspaper.

"Looks like the troops made use of this. Lucky the ceiling held. What's this blackboard? There's something written on it." Miles pointed his torch:

"'There was a young lady from Ealing
Who had a peculiar feeling
She lay on her back…'"

Miles sniggered as he read the next two lines to himself.
"No point in coming over, Pam. It's illegible."

Suddenly, Pamela screamed. "Christ. Who are they?"

Miles swung his torch round fast. The beam struck two tailor's dummies, pallid and impassive.

"They were Nanny Watson's," he said. "She did little but make dresses in her declining years. I never knew who they were for."

Two eyes gleamed.

"And there's the tiger skin."

"Let's go outside," said Pamela, stepping over rafters to reach a small door onto the roof. Something scuttled in the half-darkness.

The air outside was clear and cool. The tower of St Giles' church rose above the dark surrounding yews. Pamela steadied herself against a chimney stack. Her hand brushed the brown and leathery leaves of long-dead ivy still clinging tenaciously to the brickwork. Looking down, she could see Lorca walking away from the Stable Yard. He was smoking one of the miniature cigars he had managed to obtain in vast quantities. As Miles joined her, she said,

"There's that boy Neville. What's he up to?"

"Heading for another bullfight with Lorca perhaps. Or seeking out the feckless Filbert. I haven't seen him yet today."

Back in the attic Miles and Pamela resumed the search half-heartedly. They climbed over rolls of crumbling linoleum, shifted a pile of mouldering curtains and lighted upon a leather suitcase.

"Open it," hissed Pamela. The case was full of children's clothes. Stepping backwards, Miles felt something sharp claw at his leg. His heart missed a beat. He turned round swiftly. A mound of ghost-white antlers loomed in the torchlight. They had been removed from the Marble Hall many years before, all that remained of the famous Brockley herds that had graced the park in better times.

"A box of coat hangers, two enamel jugs and a stuffed badger," said Pamela from behind a wardrobe. "This is hopeless. Let's call it a day."

They clambered down the steep stairs from the attic to the second floor. They were filthy and breathing heavily. Pamela went into a disused bathroom and turned on a tap in the basin. The water ran brown, then orange, then finally clear. A large black spider made its escape in the nick of time. The pipes hummed painfully. The cold water and rock-hard cake of carbolic made little impression on the dirt.

"What's in here?" said Miles, pulling at a small panelled door under the stairs to the attic. It was stuck fast. He pulled again and hit his head against the sloping ceiling. He kicked the door in fury. It split and shattered. There was a sudden rush of stale air through the jagged hole. He picked carefully at the remains of the weakened door.

"Now what?" said Pamela, wiping her hands on her slacks.

"A slight accident. Defective workmanship, I shouldn't wonder. At least we can see what's there."

Several umbrellas and a rolled-up rug were balanced on a child's chair. Miles removed these and a box of photographic plates. He pulled out a tin trunk, painted black. There was a lock but no key.

"I'll get something to force it with."

"It's not locked," said Pamela, lifting the top with ease.

*

113

Horatio lay in a dwindling patch of sun on the Morning Room floor. He was taking a keen interest in what his mistress was saying.

"I can't understand how it got there. It vanished in, what, '48, '49? We thought that girl Helga had pinched it but couldn't prove anything. Just as well we didn't accuse her." The emerald ring sparkled on Pamela's hand. It was the ring she was wearing, with the matching necklace, in the de Laszlo portrait hanging on the wall a few feet away.

"You can't sell that," said Miles.

"God, no. Not for all the tea in China. But pretty odd that Helga's photograph was in the trunk with it. Torn to bits."

Miles produced the pieces from his pocket and put them loosely together on the table. A fair-haired girl with plaits and dimples was reassembled before him. She looked about sixteen.

"I'd forgotten all about her," he said. "Didn't she leave in rather a hurry?"

Before Pamela could answer Lorca ran into the room in a state of confusion.

"Sir...Lady...Brockley. Come quick. There is a man."

"What man? Where?" said Miles.

"He is in the... Grotto...yes, the Grotto. Lying down. You come with me, please."

They followed Lorca through the House and went down the steps from the terrace on the West Front. The Grotto was some distance away, the creation of an earlier Lady Brockley and her daughters. Their feat of decorating the inside with two thousand sea shells was rivalled only by that of Sir Melford, who had counted them. In his day a hermit was employed to loiter in the Grotto for the entertainment of family and friends. Now his descendant's gardener was lying face down on the stone floor.

Lorca brushed past the ferns at the entrance and poked Filbert with a stick.

"Get up. Get up."

"Stop that, Lorca," said Miles. He bent down and turned Filbert over. He recoiled sharply. "Oh Lord."

"It is Señor Filbert. He is asleep?"

"No, Lorca. I'm afraid not. There's nothing we can do. I'd better call the police."

"Did Filbert have anything with him when you found him, Lorca?" asked Pamela, glancing round the Grotto. The grubby canvas bag, from which Filbert had seemed inseparable, was nowhere to be seen.

"I don't know, I don't remember," said Lorca, looking distraught. "I did not come all the way in."

"I'd better go and see poor Mrs Filbert," said Pamela. "I don't think they have a telephone. I wonder what happened to Neville?"

11

Bleedin' 'ell, pardon my French. What does she look like? Diana frigging Dors?" Shirley Potts sat, wreathed in smoke, in the corner of the public bar of the Leg of Mutton and Cauliflower, Brockley's one and only pub. Squeezed behind a small round table with a glass of stout and a packet of Weights, she offered an opinion on anyone and anything for the few who cared to hear – and for the greater number who didn't.

"Keep your voice down," said her husband, Ron, from behind a copy of *Reynolds News*. He needn't have worried. The words washed over the pair of drinkers opposite, staring into their pints, saying nothing. The landlord went round the back to fetch another box of crisps while the girl behind the bar set about washing glasses, apparently oblivious to Shirley's comments about her newly peroxided hair.

"If you ask me, he'll get the Oscar."

"Who will?"

"That Yul Brynner."

"The bald one?"

"He shaved his head. You should have come with us."

"Where to?"

"*The King and I* in Easthampton."

"Gaumont?"

"Nah. The Teds broke the Gaumont up. Slashed the seats and pissed on the carpet. Me and Val went to the Rialto. We were singing all the way back on the bus."

"I'm glad I didn't go."

"You are a miserable so-and-so. You're still my king, though." She ruffled Ron's hair and brayed horribly.

Ron looked up from his paper. "Want another stout?"

On the station platform, Marcus removed a smut from Stella's eye with the corner of his handkerchief before they went into Brockley village.

"Let's have a quick one before we face the parents." He opened the door of the Leg of Mutton and followed Stella into the fug.

"Good God," said Shirley at the other end of the room. "I haven't seen him in a while. It's What's'isface. In the public bar! How are the mighty fallen − or is it a charitable visit?"

Ron grunted.

"Look," she hissed.

Ron looked. "It's Marcus Brockley," he said. "With a girl."

"She looks like a zombie. One of the living dead."
Shirley laughed ghoulishly.

"Do leave off."

"I thought the Brockleys offended your socialist
principles. Landed gentry, big house, inherited wealth."

"As toffs go, the Brockleys are all right. They look
after their tenants. That's more than some do."

"Mavis Collins says the House is in a right state. And
then there was that business with Tom Filbert. Who'd
be a landowner these days, eh?"

"It's lovely," said Stella, as she and Marcus emerged from
the door in the wall of the churchyard on the south-
east edge of the park. The House rose, square and pink,
beyond leafless trees and the occasional weathered urn.
A pale sun shone weakly overhead. "A real stately home.
One that's lived in." They were making their way in
single-file along the overgrown path. As they approached,
details of the House resolved, came into focus, relieving
the plain façades and bringing them to life. "It's elegant
without being flashy, if you know what I mean. I can't
think why you don't come back more often."

"Wait till you're inside," said Marcus. "Then you'll
see." They crunched onto the gravel and made for the
front door.

"They haven't fixed a date for the funeral yet," said
Pamela, standing in front of the empty fireplace in
the Morning Room. "There's to be an inquest in
Easthampton next week."

"How's Mrs Filbert taking it?" asked Marcus. He was still wearing his duffle coat, scarf and gloves.

"Bearing up. We're finding a few things for Neville around the place. There's not much left to do in the garden now until the spring."

"The last time I saw Neville he was running round in short trousers, trying to catch sparrows with a butterfly net. Mind you, that was a few years ago."

"He's changed out of all recognition in the last week or so. Suddenly grown up."

"And surprisingly competent," said Miles, coming into the Morning Room. "We like Stella. Is she feeling all right? She seems a bit pale."

"Fine. It's the face powder."

"Oh. Where is she, by the way?"

"She went outside with Lorca," said Marcus. "I brought you something." He removed a small brown envelope from his inside pocket and took out two photographs. "Max wanted you to have these." One showed Max sitting at a table in a restaurant. There was an empty glass in front of him. In the other, he was standing among trees holding a rifle. A mountain rose high in the background.

"He's looking well," said Pamela. "And much more relaxed. But surely he's been gone long enough now? Does he say when he's coming home?"

"No. It may be a while."

"Lunch will be about fifteen minutes," she said, leaving the room. In the Hall, she wiped her eyes and made for the Kitchen.

"She'll be all right," said Miles. "She misses Max a lot."

"Have you heard any more from Mrs Finch?"

"Not since March. I went to see her. I hope I made the position clear."

Lorca had set up the target on the lawn below the Terrace. He brushed off the cobwebs roughly, removed some dangling pieces of straw, and walked away from it. Picking up the wooden bow from the grass, he inserted the bowstring into the notch of one of the arrows standing in the long tom that served as a quiver. He pulled back the string and let go, propelling the arrow towards the target. It was not even close. Horatio obligingly retrieved the missile and dropped it at Lorca's feet. He tried again and caught the edge of the white outermost ring of the target. Stella applauded politely from her vantage point on the Terrace.

"Can I have a go?" she said, as Lorca struck the black twice in succession.

Her first arrow struck the red ring, her second the gold in the centre of the target.

"Bull's eye!" said Marcus, suddenly appearing above the balustrade. "I've been sent to summon you to lunch."

Stella handed the bow to the despondent Lorca and followed Marcus inside. Horatio ambled behind them. Lorca muttered to himself as he tried again. White...black...black... . Pulling the string back as far as he could he sent the arrow way past the target. He had not seen the peacock advancing jerkily towards him.

The arrow struck the unfortunate bird in the chest. He went to recover it. "Oh no," he cried, when he saw what he had done. "Oh no." He began to panic. He ran backwards and forwards trying to think what to do. "Sir Brockley kill me if he find out."

He threw the bow to the ground and picked up the peacock with some difficulty. A sudden gust of wind caught the tail, propelling him round in a half-circle. He staggered in the direction of the Ice House in the stand of beeches a few hundred yards to the left of the Grotto. Built of brick and limestone at the same time as Brockley House, the Ice House had long been disused. He edged in with his unwieldy cargo and placed it carefully on the cold stone floor. He shivered. He grabbed the arrow, put his hand over his eyes, took a deep breath and pulled.

He wiped the arrow on the grass on his way back. Gathering up target, bow and remaining arrows, he staggered back to the tack room and left them in a corner where he had found them. In his own room he finished off the bottle of Sir Miles' brandy he kept there and wondered what to do.

"Lady Brockley," said Lorca later, "ees my birthday. I cook a special meal for you and Sir Brockley. Ees paella, like my mother used to make."

"How thoughtful," said Pamela. "And many happy returns. Do you have all the ingredients?"

12

It was a bleak December day. Miles leaned on a post beside the rough chalk track as he waited for Horatio to catch up. His smooth-handled walking stick hung from the top of the fence, swaying gently. From his position on the high ground he surveyed the House and surrounding parkland. Even in its skeletal winter form the park was calm, peaceful, soothing. From up here, it all seemed right, everything under control and perfectly related, not a tree out of place.

As Horatio snuffled up and flopped at his feet, Miles saw a column of blue-grey smoke rising from somewhere below. He assumed, without thinking, that Filbert was burning something in the garden. Then he remembered. Filbert would be lighting no more fires.

Miles set off down the track towards the House. The smoke was becoming thicker. It looked as though it was coming from the direction of the Stable Yard. It was. He walked faster and broke into a run, leaving

Horatio to make his own way back. The wind was getting up. The charred remains of paper that Lorca had used to start a bonfire were floating about the yard as Miles rushed in. Pamela, Neville and Lorca himself were already there with brooms and buckets, dousing the burning straw and what remained of the lower half of the tack room door. When the fire was out, Miles looked round to inspect the damage. They had been lucky. Lorca was abjectly apologetic and blamed the wind. In the pile of sodden debris swept into the middle of the yard there appeared to be some feathers. A lone peacock called mournfully from the Terrace.

Miles was perched on the top of the Library steps a little later, reading a copy of *Punch*. The wind moaned in the chimney. The newspaper stuffed up it to reduce draughts agitated but stayed in place. Gilt lettering caught the light of the standard lamp, bindings of volumes rarely touched and never read. Miles adjusted the scarf round his neck and chuckled quietly. Pamela looked up from a green leather armchair, avoiding Oscar's glassy gaze, and said, "Why are you wearing odd socks?"

"I could only find one of each: one red and one yellow. At least they brighten the place up a bit."

"I suppose so. Do you remember Max said he missed the winter in England? There are no seasons where he is, apart from rains and things."

"He must have forgotten what it's like," said Miles. "*When icicles hang by the wall…*" he began. "How does it go?"

"*When icicles hang by the wall / And Dick the shepherd blows his nail / And Tom bears logs into the hall…*"

Pamela faltered. "Oh," she said. "Poor Filbert. Did I say? The verdict was misadventure. All pretty gruesome. Neville broke his silence and said something about seeing his father slip on wet grass and fall into the ha-ha."

"After a bottle or two, no doubt. How on earth did he end up in the Grotto?"

"Neville is supposed to have helped him out at one end of the ha-ha and supported him to the Grotto."

"Why there? It's a long way."

"Probably because he could lie down in the dry without being seen. Or so he thought."

"He was obviously still alive at that point."

"So it seems."

"What happened to Neville?"

"He said he panicked when his father collapsed in the Grotto. Ran off to Brockley Woods. He wasn't at home when I went to tell Mary Filbert that day. His mother didn't know where he was."

"Hm," said Miles, landing in the chair next to Pamela.

"The funeral's on Monday of next week at St Giles. We shall need to be there."

"Yes. And Lorca presumably. He's finding Neville quite a help."

"Are we going to be able to keep Neville on?"

"For the time being but we'll need to find a gardener by the spring. Assuming we're still here then."

"Why shouldn't we be?"

"Paget says there's no joy on the grant front. He says

why don't we stock the park with deer and produce venison. I hardly think so."

"Why not? We had deer in the park before the war."

"Paget's talking about a proper commercial operation. We've no staff and no facilities and no money for investment. I don't see Mr Stoat giving us a loan."

"What about the Heritage Commission? It's taken on Kendon Manor. Rex and Aurelia have a house in the grounds."

"The Commission doesn't take anything on these days without a decent endowment. We can't provide an endowment and if we could we'd be all right anyway."

"Sell off the land by the station?"

"We've been through all that. I can't keep the estate intact if we sell bits off."

"Let's have a chat with Marco when we see him at Christmas. He needs a say in this too."

"All right."

"Miles, I don't like this any more than you do. But things will have to change if you want them to stay as they are."

Part Four

The Present

1

Why not just ask someone why they changed the upstairs route to cut out the Yellow Room?" said Duncan. The table in the Tea Room at Brockley House rocked gently on the uneven floor.

"I've tried that," said Jessica. "The stewards I've asked either don't know or aren't saying. One just said it was a private apartment and went off to help some children find a badger."

She hesitated for a moment, then dived into her bag. She removed a small maroon leather box. It was badly scuffed but it was possible to make out the letter P, or possibly B, in the middle of the lid. She opened the box to reveal a silver brooch, pinned to a frayed silk cushion. The brooch was in the form of a badger. The eyes – or rather eye: only one was visible – appeared to be of sapphire.

"It's like the badger on the back of the chairs in the Marble Hall," said Duncan.

"And on the dinner service in the Dining Room."

"Where on earth did you get it?"

"My grandmother left it to me. She died a couple of months ago."

"Oh. I'm sorry. Nothing to indicate where the brooch came from?"

"It was just in this box. The guidebook, the old one, came from my grandmother too. Perhaps she came to Brockley once. It was written by Lady Pamela, you know. It's rather poignant. She talks about the great clump of elms you can see from the Morning Room windows and how the rooks have nested there for generations."

"I don't remember seeing any elms."

"They had to be cut down, along with all the others in the park. Dutch elm disease. It's mentioned in the new guide."

"What a shame. I wonder where the rooks went?"

Jessica shrugged her shoulders.

"Did Lady P say anything about the Yellow Room?"

"Not much. It was the bedroom shared by her sons at one time. Marcus and Max. M and M," she added softly, almost inaudibly. As she picked up the slim green guide a small piece of newspaper fell out and landed on the table. Duncan picked it up and gave it to her.

"This doesn't seem to fit at all," she said, unfolding the cutting carefully. "*Easthampton Advertiser.* 3 June 1953. 'Coronation Tragedy in Brockley. Yesterday's Coronation Day celebrations in Brockley village came to a sad conclusion with the death of eleven-year old William Smith from Rodway Cottages. His body was discovered beside the River Brock under the bridge on the Easthampton Road. The police say that his neck had been broken. An investigation is under way.' That's it."

Duncan came back with fresh supplies of tea and coffee. The visitor hordes were beginning to subside. He squeezed into his place and said,

"I was thinking. In the queue. Can't your parents shed any light on this?"

"I doubt it. I've never heard them mention Brockley. They hadn't been born themselves in 1953."

"Your grandmother might have mentioned something."

"Not that I remember. She was very cagey about the past."

"Grandfather?"

"That's just it. I never met him. My grandmother was unmarried and brought my mother up by herself. She never talked about him."

"What about your mother's birth certificate or marriage certificate? Wouldn't they have to give the father's name?"

"I don't think they do. My mother's maiden name was the same as my grandmother's.

"What was that?"

"Finch."

"Why don't you put on the brooch?" said Duncan as they were preparing to go back into the House to look at the Teniers. She did not mind seeing them again, now that the crowds had subsided, and she rather enjoyed the company.

"I don't really wear brooches."

"It belongs here."

"It's rather old-fashioned. And it doesn't go with what I'm wearing."

"See if anybody notices."

Jessica pinned it with some reluctance to the lapel of her linen jacket. The badger looked entirely at home. She and Duncan went out of the Tea Room, into the Stable Yard and through a door that took them into the Kitchen corridor. They were aiming for the staircase that would bring them up on the ground floor between the Dining Room and the Marble Hall. Duncan paused to admire the old wire bell-pull system that had enabled the family to summon the servants in years gone by. A little further on he caught a glimpse of copper jelly moulds gleaming through the Kitchen door above a blackened range. He dodged a party emerging from the Butler's Pantry and caught up with Jessica near the foot of the staircase. She was looking at the truncated oars fixed to the wall. They were dark blue with gold chevrons.

"See the name. 'Stroke. M M St J Brockley. Trinity 1949.' And again: 'Hilary 1950.' That must be Marcus," she said with authority. "He was at St Luke's. How funny."

As Duncan was about to ask why Marcus Brockley's Oxford college should give rise to mirth he became aware of a grey-haired man staring at them from the staircase. The man came down a few steps but said nothing. His eyes focused on Jessica and on her brooch. His face was drained of colour. He looked as though he had seen a ghost. He came closer.

"Excuse me, Miss. But where did you get that?" he said, pointing at the brooch. "If you don't mind my asking." He was wearing a badge with his name on it. It said, NEVILLE FILBERT. "The silver badger. It's been missing for…over fifty years."

"How on earth can you say that after so long?" Duncan intruded protectively. "Mr Filbert."

"It's all right," said Jessica quietly. "I'd like to hear this."

"I'd know it anywhere. It was a favourite of her ladyship's. Lady Pamela. She was very upset when it disappeared."

"Were you at Brockley? Back then?"

"I used to play here. Me and my sisters. My father was the gardener in Sir Miles' time."

"But you could only have been a small boy," said Duncan. "How could you remember it so clearly?"

"We used to admire it. And it looks just like the other badgers round the place. You can blame Sir Matthew for that. It was his idea of a joke." He paused and turned to Jessica. "You know…may I?"

Neville Filbert took the glossy guidebook from her, turned straight to the de Laszlo portrait of Lady Pamela and held it up to Jessica. The resemblance was striking.

"Is there somewhere we can go, Mr Filbert?" said Jessica. "I think we need to have a conversation."

Duncan wondered what to do. Perhaps he should go now and leave them to it. This was nothing to do with him. He had only just met her. But he had been happy to listen to what she had to say. More than happy. He wanted to hear more.

"You're welcome to join us," said Jessica softly. It was a request not an invitation. She wanted him there.

Neville led them up the stairs, through the Marble Hall and out of the front door. He swung left away from the drive on a narrow path that curled round groups of trees and assorted statuary. A solitary peacock paused to let them pass. The ground on one side fell away towards the Lake, shimmering in the afternoon haze. They overtook visitors undertaking the Long Walk round the grounds and cut between patches of hawthorn and spindle. Clusters of berries shone in the sun.

Neville brought them to a halt before a door set in a mellow brick wall. The door was marked PRIVATE. An unruly red rose trailed across it. He took out a large key from his jacket pocket and turned it sharply in the lock. The door whined open. Jessica and Duncan ducked under the rose and followed him into the Walled Garden. He took care to lock the door behind them.

"The secret garden," said Jessica, just to herself. She was hot and pink and out of breath. Neville dragged some chairs into the dappled shade of apple trees. He removed his jacket and Jessica removed hers. The warm air hung still and heavy, as if trapped by the high walls. There was a sense of time suspended, of the garden as a refuge, cut off from the world outside. Jessica shifted awkwardly on her chair, not sure whether to take the initiative or wait for Neville to come to the point. She played it by ear.

"Once upon a time," said Neville, "this was the nerve centre of the estate. It supplied fruit and vegetables and flowers for the House throughout the year. And for the markets in London too. Hard to believe now, isn't it?"

Jessica and Duncan slowly took in what remained of the old kitchen garden – the broken glasshouses and collapsed cold-frames, the rusty pipework, the paths and borders choked with weeds.

"See there," said Neville, pointing to the south-facing wall pitted by hundreds of nail holes. "There used to be peaches and nectarines, trained against the wall. Not in my time. Long, long ago. Brockley fruit used to be famous. Won prizes for grapes and melons at the Royal Horticultural Society shows. We've got the records in the House. Six different kinds of cabbage; five of broccoli; peas, beans, sprouts, cauliflower, spinach. You name it, they grew it."

"Can't it be restored?" asked Jessica.

"There's talk from time to time but what's the point? It's a relic of a bygone age. Perhaps it's best to leave it like that."

Yet here and there were signs of activity, of grass scythed and nettles felled, of brambles cut and bindweed held at bay. And the wooden chairs weren't old at all.

"My son and grandson do a bit from time to time. Mostly in the area near the door. It's a place to come when you want to get away. The Commission doesn't mind."

A dragonfly darted towards them, hovered for an instant and darted off again. Jessica shuffled her feet while Duncan stared at the ground. She prompted Neville gently about Miles and Pamela.

"They were always good to me," he said, "especially after my father died. It must have been hard for them, seeing the place falling about their ears. I helped out in the gardens but it was a losing battle. They kept me on when they moved to The Sett. That was much more manageable."

"What about the sons?" said Jessica. "Marcus and Max."

"We didn't see much of them, what with one thing and another. National Service and so on. They both went to live abroad. How did you say you came by that brooch, Miss?" The badger looked subdued in the shade.

"My grandmother left it to me in her will."

"I wonder how she got it."

"Not a clue. I don't remember her wearing it at all."

"Did she know Brockley?"

"I think she must have been here because I found this in her cottage," said Jessica, delving into her bag.

"I haven't seen one of those for a long time." Neville slowly turned the pages of the dark green guide and gave it back to her.

"My grandmother underlined the Yellow Room on the plan. At least, I assume it was her. It was open to the public then but it isn't now. Do you know why?"

"When Sir Miles died Lady Pamela moved back to the House. She was getting on herself and The Sett was too big for her. So she had an apartment on the first floor. When she died the Commission let it to another tenant and expanded it to include the Yellow Room. It was nothing special."

"The steward in the Library said the tenant knew the House in the 1950s," said Jessica.

"Yes. I believe he did. Do you mind my asking what your grandmother's name was, Miss?"

"It was May. May Finch."

Neville did not reply. His face impassive, expressionless. Perhaps just a flicker in the eyes.

"Do you know the name?" asked Duncan.

"It's hard to say after all this time. Well, I must be going. I'm back on duty in fifteen minutes."

As Neville got to his feet and started to retrieve his jacket from the back of the chair Jessica removed something from an envelope in her bag.

"Do you recognise this man, Mr Filbert?"

Neville took the photograph from her and looked at it.

"I don't think I can help you," he said quickly. "I ought to be getting back."

On the other side of the garden door he said, "Is there some way I can get hold of you, Miss? Just in case anything comes to mind."

Jessica gave him one of her business cards. He put it in his top pocket and rushed off.

2

That evening, Jessica sat alone at the circular dining table in her east London flat. It was hot and humid inside and all the windows were open as far as they would go in a forlorn attempt to catch the stiffening breeze. A stray carrier bag, snared in the cherry tree at the front, rustled persistently, as if whispering to her a message she could not understand. She disposed quickly of quiche and salad and a raspberry yoghurt, and cleared a space on the table. In the middle she put the scuffed red box that housed the badger brooch.

She lifted the lid. The badger's sapphire eye caught the light and sparkled. Around the box, in the shape of a horseshoe, she assembled the photograph she had found slipped inside the old green guide, the copies of the two photographs briefly liberated from Brockley, and the glossy guide to the House, open at the picture of Lady Pamela. Behold the badger, behold the man – or woman. The conclusion was inescapable.

The prospect was daunting, darkly exciting. But where did it leave her? Neville Filbert, she thought, clearly knew more than he was letting on. He said he knew Brockley in Sir Miles' day so he must have known his sons, Marcus and Max. And he must have recognised the photograph she showed him. Even she had done that. How much did he know? Then there was her mother. When should she tell her? How would she take to the news? But was there really any point in saying anything? It was all so long ago. In any case, she needed proof, not just a strong suspicion.

She looked again at the photographs. They were a striking family. Marcus must be in his mid-seventies by now and Max only a little younger. The guide said that Marcus was living with his family in the United States. The family must surely be grown up. Maybe there were grandchildren too. She flicked to the family tree at the back of the guide. There, at the bottom. Marcus (eleventh Baronet) married Vanessa Peters in 1960. Three children: Matthew (born 1963), Melford (1968) and Melissa (1973). No mention of grandchildren. But what of Max? The guide said nothing about him, apart from his name and date of birth in the family tree. No marriage and no offspring were recorded. Neville Filbert had said that Max had gone abroad too but not where he went.

She turned the guide back to the picture of Lady Pamela. She held the page in place with a couple of books and went to her desk in the spare room next door. In the third drawer down she found two photographs of her mother in her twenties. She was on the beach, holding a frisbee, laughing at someone or something out of sight. Nice to see her looking relaxed and happy. It was pretty unusual these days. She put the photographs on the dining room table with the other pictures and stood back. Not quite so compelling, perhaps lacking the finer features, but still not much doubt. Now what?

She sat down at the table and stared at the Howard Hodgkin print on the wall. Its bands and splodges and swirls of colour relieved the bland magnolia of the previous occupier that she had always meant to change. She still had the paint cards from Decorators' World but the more she looked at them the less she could distinguish between the shades. The fine gradations of colour made her brain ache.

She wished there was someone she could confide in, to talk to about what to do. She spent her professional life giving advice to others. Now she needed some herself.... . She had friends, of course. Well, a few, but she doubted that they could really help. Anyway, it did not seem right to air family secrets in front of others. And yet her mother was the last person she wanted to let in on this now. She would lose control of the situation completely. Her father? Jack The Lad? No chance. May's simple shoebox, she thought, could turn out more like Pandora's box.

And then there was Duncan. It had been nice to share things with him, to have his quiet support at a difficult moment. But that was at Brockley, a chance encounter in the Tea Room. She had only met him once. He was a complete stranger really. Only, it did not feel like that. There was something about him. She had been comfortable with him. They spoke the same language. And he did not try too hard; he just seemed natural. When they had parted that afternoon she had promised to keep him in touch, to let him know if she had further and better particulars, as she put it. She had his e-mail address but what could she say?

Maybe he would get in touch with her. Just for a drink. He had her card. But why should he? He was probably married anyway. Almost certainly. Bound to be at that age. Difficult for him to get away, even if he wanted to. Still, he'd gone to Brockley by himself... . She got up, went over to the window and stood for a long time staring at the dark shapes of trees flailing in the breeze, her forehead pressed against the glass.

A week or so later, Jessica was leaning on the imitation granite work surface in the kitchen at Quarrenden and Cox waiting for the kettle to boil. The urn was temporarily out of commission, the handle having been wrenched off by Clyde Pitmaston in a misguided attempt to demonstrate its strength and indestructibility. A large notice had been stuck on the door of the fridge warning all users that it was to be cleaned over the coming weekend and that any items left therein would be disposed of forthwith.

She was enjoying five minutes' peace. The telephone had not stopped ringing and Clyde kept droning on about hang gliding, wind surfing, and the Red Hot Chili Peppers.

She was intercepted by Linda on the way back to her office.

"You had a phone call."

"Not the Environment Agency again?"

"No. It was a strange man." Linda glanced at her pad. "He said could you come on Sunday afternoon and bring the brooch. Then he rang off. His name was Filbert."

"Did he leave his number?"

"He put the phone down before I could ask. Sorry."

Jessica parked her Peugeot in the car park at Brockley dead on opening time. It was just as well she had checked the trains. There were no trains. The line between Ridgewell and Easthampton was closed for engineering works over the whole weekend. The replacement bus service took more than twice as long.

At the pavilion mere mention of the name of Filbert was enough to speed her through without a ticket. Two pigeons nodded approvingly from the elder by the gate and continued to pluck the berries methodically. An uncertain grey day was turning into a sunny afternoon. It was mid-September.

As she walked towards the House she again felt guilty about Duncan. She had promised to let him know if there was any news. Not that there had been, really. And she had not heard from him, either. Even so, she could have done with some moral support today. She dealt with senior barristers and demanding clients without turning a hair. Now she felt nervous and slightly sick. She had no idea what to expect, what Neville wanted to say. And why did he want to see the badger brooch again? But she could not have declined to come. She needed to know.

Skittering across the gravel in front of the House, she went past the entrance in the direction of the Stable Yard. The red and pink heads of sedums in the flower beds were thick with butterflies. She turned the corner by the recently planted hornbeam hedge and made for what an American woman with the same idea called 'the little girls' room'. Just inside the House, Jessica again uttered the password 'Filbert'. The stern visage of the matron at the door collapsed into a beam. She withdrew her ticket-taking hand and pointed towards a small mahogany door at the foot of the wooden staircase near the Morning Room. Jessica gulped, knocked and waited. There was no answer. She knocked again, harder this time, paused and turned the handle.

A newspaper was open at the racing page on a battered pine table in the middle of the room. An empty mug stood nearby. It was badly in need of cleaning. A portable television flickered on the top of a low cupboard. The place appeared to be deserted. But thoughts of the *Mary Celeste* were rapidly dispelled as Neville Filbert emerged backwards from the walk-in larder clutching a large packet of chocolate biscuits. He turned round, started and composed himself.

"I thought you'd come," he said, putting the biscuits on the table. "Is the other one with you?"

"It's just me," said Jessica brightly.

"Good. I think that's as well. Some things are best kept in the family, so to speak."

Neville slipped into his jacket and smoothed his hair. He made for the door, beckoning her to follow.

"Where are we going?"

"Upstairs."

"Can't we talk here?"

But Neville was already through the door and into the corridor. He locked the door behind them and strode across the marble floor of the Hall. Up the stone staircase on the other side, two steps at a time. Jessica struggled to keep up. Where was he taking her? Was she making a mistake? She was beginning to lose her nerve. He stopped at the top of the stairs and removed a large bunch of keys from his jacket pocket. After swift but careful scrutiny he selected a small brass key and inserted it into the lock of the door marked PRIVATE.

"Nearly there, Miss."

"Does anyone else know where we're going?" She felt the panic rising. Should she run back down while the going was good?

"Oh yes. That's why we're here."

The corridor on the other side was dark. The air smelled stale, fusty. Neville pressed a time-switch and a light came on, a single naked bulb dangling from the high ornamented ceiling. At the end of the corridor there was a window, shrouded in a heavy velvet curtain that excluded the light of day. A door on the left-hand side was slightly ajar. Jessica could make out a high-backed winged armchair and the corner of a bed.

"Did you bring the brooch?"

She said "yes" in a small voice. He knocked gently on the door on the right, the door of the Yellow Room.

He interpreted the noise from within as permission to enter and turned the handle.

"This is Miss Jessica Tate," he said in the direction of the chair by the fireplace.

She moved slowly towards it.

"Miss Tate, may I introduce Mr Max Brockley."

Part Five

1954

1

Max yawned loudly, stretched and clambered out of the deep armchair in which he had fallen asleep. His dark hair was sticking up at the back. The flowered chintz of the chairs in the comfortable sitting room reminded him of an English country vicarage. Roses? Paeonies? It was hard to tell. The tea that the house boy, Joseph, had brought him was now lukewarm. Max drained the bone china cup in a single gulp, stood up and went out onto the veranda.

The air was crisp and clear. The silence of the still afternoon was broken by the loud chatter of weaver birds in the trees near the bungalow. A metallic flash signalled a sunbird by the bougainvillea trailing, purple and orange, over the side of the veranda. Max leaned against a brick pillar and looked into the distance, down past the smooth green lawn and beds of fiery cannas, past the barbed wire fence at the bottom of the garden to the dense forest beyond. He did not notice the arrival of James Campbell-Hill, a tall man with a healthy tan and brown-gold hair.

"Habari?"

Max started. "Mzuri sana," he said, recovering his composure.

"Very good," said James. "Sorry to give you a fright. Welcome to Kenya Colony." He shook Max's hand quickly but firmly. "The last time I saw you was on the front steps at Brockley. You were going back to school the next day. Any sign of Molly?"

"She went into Nawiri."

"Let's hope she's not long, the way things are now."

"She had Joseph with her."

"I'm afraid that's no guarantee of anything. She ought to take a pistol. How long are you with us? Miles wasn't entirely clear in his letter."

"Just till things blow over. I'm due up at St Luke's in October."

"Ah, St Luke's," said James distantly. "That's where I first met your father. Must have been about thirty-five years ago. How are things at Brockley?"

"Crumbling gently. The parents are existing hand-to-mouth as usual. They're still looking for a replacement for Prodgers after that business with the grocer's boy in the game larder. Rumour has it that a Spaniard's in contention, would you believe? Still, Brockley's not my problem. That'll be for Marcus to worry about, if the place is still standing by then. He spends most of his time in London."

"It's still your home. It's a fixed point, somewhere

to go back to. Kenya's full of younger sons who left because they wouldn't inherit but they still talk about England as home and still go back from time to time. You're lucky. Monkwell's been turned into a school. Brockley's almost home for me now."

Molly marched into the bungalow with Joseph behind her carrying the baskets. He looked older than his fifty years. He paused at the threshold to remove his sandals and went off with his load towards the kitchen, where Edward, the cook, was contemplating the meal ahead.

"Chai," bellowed Molly, as an afterthought.

"Ndio, Memsahib," returned Joseph quietly. The whites of his eyes were yellowed and bloodshot.

Molly breezed onto the veranda, her shoes and slacks bearing a pinkish tinge from the red dust on the streets of Nawiri.

"Tea is on its way," she announced. "This was at the post office." She thrust an airmail envelope at Max and flopped onto a lounger.

"For me? I've only just arrived." Max turned the envelope over. "It's from Marcus. I'll read it later," he said, putting the letter in his shirt pocket.

"Max is already speaking Swahili," said James.

"Only a few words. There was a list of useful words and phrases in the guidebook I was reading on the train from Mombasa."

"I'll teach you," said Molly. "Swahili's not too difficult. Kikuyu's fiendish."

"The DC's managed," said James. "He says dealing

with the Kikuyu in their own language makes all the difference."

"That's the District Commissioner," Molly whispered to Max, as Joseph, now resplendent in red fez and long white kanzu, brought the tea on an oval tray and laid it out silently on the bamboo table.

"It's getting chilly," said Molly later. "Let's go inside."

"I thought we were almost on the Equator," said Max.

"We are but it's over six thousand feet up here in the Highlands," said James.

"It's the *White* Highlands," corrected Molly, "and we intend to keep it that way."

"Ssh. Pas devant. Asante, Joseph."

James stood in front of the fire blazing in the big stone fireplace. A stack of freshly chopped cedar logs stood to one side. "The Highlands are a European reserve," he said, "apart from the townships. Land cannot be transferred to Africans…"

"Or Indians," put in Molly.

"Isn't that a bit hard to justify?" said Max. "Not letting people own land in their own country."

"If it was open to all comers the Europeans would be forced out," said Molly. "How would that help anyone? The Africans couldn't run a farm in a month of Sundays and if the Indians bought the place up the Africans would be no better off. Things should be left as they are."

"Come and help me check the windows, Max," said James after a brief but awkward silence. "We need to make sure the wire netting's still in place. We do this every evening in case it's been tampered with."

"Who would do that?"

"With luck, no one. But all the attacks on Europeans round here have been by the servants themselves or carried out with their active support. Our friends the Sandersons were hacked to death by their own houseboy last month. He'd been with them fifteen years."

Joseph lit the Tilly lamps and drew the curtains while the others sipped the gins and tonic he had brought them.

"Kwa heri, Memsahib. Kwa heri, Bwana. Kwa heri, Bwana Max."

When Joseph had left, James locked the outer doors. Molly went to the kitchen to cook the trout that Edward had prepared earlier. That was how it was these days. It was a bore but she could not take the risk.

Two alsatians lay in front of the fire, alert to the slightest sound from outside. James put on the World Service and disappeared while Max studied stiffly posed photographs of the Campbell-Hill twins, taken in a Nairobi studio the previous year. Susan and Jennifer, Molly had said, both now at university in England. Max wondered if their paths would cross.

James returned holding two revolvers.

"You'll need this," he said, handing Max a .38. "I assume you can handle it after your National Service. Molly has hers with her. Keep it with you at all times."

"Even in bed?"

"Especially in bed."

That night, Max lay in his room in the extension of the bungalow that the Campbell-Hills had christened Xanadu. He pulled the blanket over him and re-read the letter. Although it had his brother's name and address on the back of the envelope it was from his mother, Lady Pamela. They had agreed that all communications between Brockley and Nawiri should be via Marcus in London. It seemed safer that way.

2

"Hodi, Bwana Max." Joseph came into the bedroom next morning with a cup of tea.

"Asante sana."

Joseph picked up Max's shoes and left. Max stretched and parted the curtains. He could see nothing. Through the mist that had come down from the forest, he could hear the raucous sound of hornbills above the gentle gurgling of the stream outside his window.

"James is an early riser," said Molly, helping herself to a few more slices of paw-paw while Edward made the scrambled egg and bacon. "He's gone to the Waterbuck to sort out a safari for some of the guests. They keep on coming despite the Emergency. He'll be back in time for lunch. We're having a few people over."

Once the mist had cleared, Molly and Max went down the rough stone steps into the garden. Cape chestnuts with mauve blossoms rose high above them. The garden boy, Charles, was clearing grass slowly with his panga.

"Vicious-looking weapon," said Max.

"A Mau Mau favourite. It can inflict horrendous damage. Let's not talk about it."

They stood on a rustic bridge over the stream. Maidenhair fern grew from the mossy stones along its edge.

"We thought you might help out at the hotel," said Molly. James'll show you the ropes. It's hard to say who's more troublesome – the guests or the staff. We had an American the other week demanding to see tigers. Nothing would persuade him there weren't any in Kenya. Fortunately, he went to sleep after his fifth whisky and forgot all about it. How are you for money?"

"My father opened an account for me with the Standard Bank of South Africa. Put a fair amount in it, too. Said a new roof would have to wait."

Molly said nothing. Neither did Charles, who had been watching them quietly. He put his panga down and picked up a rake.

Molly did the introductions before lunch. "Bill Sharp you know. He owns a coffee plantation up the road at Mweiga. Roger Lewis is Dalgety's man at Nakuru, when he's not playing polo at Njoro."

Max smiled politely.

"Alison and Peter Fox have a farm at Naro Moru. And this is their niece, Bryony." The guests were suntanned and relaxed, making Max feel pale and unhealthy.

Molly ushered everyone onto the veranda where Joseph was waiting to dispense drinks.

"Did you fly?" asked Roger.

"I came by boat – Union-Castle to Mombasa – then the train. It's not exactly *The Flying Scotsman* but I saw my first elephant and zebra out of the window and lots of brown things with horns that I couldn't identify. Bill Sharp picked me up from the station in Nairobi and brought me here."

"With a few stops on the way," added Molly.

"I had to change some library books at Muthaiga for Daphne so I thought I'd show Max round." Bill sounded defensive.

"Is there another library at Thika?"

"We stopped at the Blue Posts for a Tusker. It seemed a pity not to let Max see the Falls."

Max thought back to his visit to the Muthaiga Country Club the morning before. After the noise of Nairobi, the Club was disconcertingly quiet. While Bill sorted out the books for his wife, Max walked slowly around the gardens, admiring the lush vegetation against the pink pebbledash of the Club buildings. As he reached the croquet lawn a game turned nasty. The peace was shattered by the crack of mallet against mallet and furious accusations of cheating. He thought better of separating the warring women and declined their attempts to draw him into arbitration. He thought idly of the flamingos he had been assured were to be found in quantity in the Rift Valley. Pretty uncooperative mallets, as Alice had found. He had no information about the distribution of hedgehogs.

A well-lubricated tour of the clocks and crests of the members' bar was followed, at Bill's insistence, by snooker in the games room. As he was chalking his cue before tackling the blue, Bill turned to Max and said, "Steer clear of the local girls, won't you. You might get more than you bargained for. Take it from me. Not a word to Daphne."

"We came out by flying boat in 1938," said Alison Fox. "Imperial Airways. We landed on Lake Naivasha. The service doesn't run any more. Rather a shame."

"I love the lake," said Bryony. "You must let me take you there."

"Give Max a chance," said Molly. "He's only just arrived."

"Max. That's rather a wicked name," said Bryony. "Like Max de Winter. Are you wicked?"

"Er…"

"'Last night I dreamt I went to Manderley again'," said James in a ghastly falsetto.

"Thank you, James," said Molly. "That will do. Let's go through to the dining room."

"It's Podo," said James, with an air of pride.

"I'm not with you," said Max.

"The table. It's made from a single plank of Podo

wood from the slopes of Mount Elgon. That's on the border with Uganda."

"Very impressive. It must have been an enormous tree." Max tried to avoid Bryony's eye as Joseph served the soup.

"You've come to Kenya at a difficult time," said Peter Fox. "Mau Mau want to drive us out. They say we've stolen Kikuyu land."

"It's a lie," said Molly, sitting bolt upright. "Most of the White Highlands was never Kikuyu territory anyway. And the European farms are packed out with Kikuyu squatters."

"I wonder if we aren't fighting a losing battle, living on borrowed time and all that," said James. "Not a popular view but we can't pretend there isn't a land problem. The reserves are bursting at the seams. It might defuse things to make them a bit bigger."

"And reward Mau Mau for their efforts? It's unthinkable."

"Molly's right," said Bill. "We can't give in to terrorists. And where would it stop? It's the settlers who worked to create something out of nothing, against the odds. Drought, rain, rinderpest, locusts, rust…you can't expect us to throw it all away. Besides, there's a new generation of Europeans growing up who were born here. When they say 'home' they mean Kenya, not England."

"This is not just about hanging on to land, Max," said Roger. "It's about defending civilised values and our way of life."

*

Joseph cleared away the soup plates while Edward brought in the lamb, potatoes and peas. When they had left the room, Alison said breathily,

"Have you heard? The Nesbits have sacked all their Kikuyu servants for taking the oath. They had a tip-off from the police. They're taking on some Samburu boys instead."

"What's the oath?" said Max.

"To kill a white man if ordered to do so by Mau Mau – on pain of death."

"They have ceremonies in huts in the forest at the dead of night."

"They have to drink goat's blood," said Bryony.

"And worse," said Roger. "Much worse."

"They're savages," said Alison. "Monsters."

"Mentally ill, if you ask me. Diseased. Pass the potatoes, James."

"Are you glad you came, Max?"

The shot rang out while coffee was being served. A single shot at the front of the house. The assembled company started but remained calm. Everyone was in the sitting room except Bill. James picked up his revolver and ran to the front door. Bryony moved closer to Max.

When James opened the door he saw Bill crouching on the ground with his back to the bungalow. Bill turned and stood up as he heard James call his name.

"Puff adder," said Bill cheerfully. "I was out here for

a quick fag and met this chap." He held the snake up by its tail.

A little later, Max and Bryony sat beside the stream running through the garden. A gentle breeze played with Bryony's straw-coloured hair. Slowly, reflectively, she said,

> " '*And there were gardens bright with sinuous rills*
> *Where blossomed many an incense-bearing tree;*' "

" '*And here,*' " said Max,

> "'*were forests ancient as the hills,*
> *Enfolding sunny spots of greenery.*'"

"Touché! You did it at school too. I don't think Coleridge came to the Highlands of Kenya."

"Don't let Molly hear you call them that. She insists on calling them the White Highlands."

"They're like Canute, this lot," said Bryony. "Trying to turn back the tide. They can't see what's going on around them. I'd give it five years, ten at the most."

"Then what?"

"Who knows? If they've any sense, they'll forget the past and all work together, African, Indian and European."

"A bit optimistic, when people are being hacked to death."

"The Emergency won't last forever," said Bryony. "Anyway, it's mostly Africans that are being killed left, right and centre, though you wouldn't think so, listening to people round here."

"Someone did mention there was a spot of bother at a place called Lari last year."

"A massacre, not far from Nairobi. Mau Mau wiped out nearly a hundred Kikuyu loyalists."

"Good God. Sounds more like civil war."

"It is, though the buffoons in Government House say it's merely a 'disturbance'. Why don't we go into Nawiri?"

"What, now?"

"Why not?"

3

Bryony drove slowly past the flame trees in the drive, out along the corrugated murram track that led to the township of Nawiri. A low cloud of red dust rose behind the car, her uncle's Ford V8. She stopped to let Max follow the progress of some black-and-white Colobus monkeys high in the trees above. A little further on, in a clearing off to the left, was a group of round thatched huts. A few chickens scratched about in front of the nearest hut, where a small boy was milking a cow. As they went past, Max saw a face looking at the car through a gap in the maize. It was Charles, the garden boy from Xanadu.

Bryony parked under one of the jacarandas forming an avenue in the main street of Nawiri. The street was lined with mostly Indian-owned dukas, small shops selling a variety of goods. At the Good Luck Stores in the square Bryony paused to buy a packet of

Churchman's while Max went to inspect the small fruit and vegetable market opposite. Passion fruit and mango he had never seen before. He guessed the paw-paw from the slices he had had at breakfast. The bananas were easy but much smaller than any he had previously encountered. As he loitered by a pile of pineapples he was surrounded by a cluster of small children shouting 'Jambo'. They looked up at him with big eyes and held out their hands.

"Don't give them anything," said Bryony, putting the cigarettes in her bag. "Once you start you won't be able to stop."

The group followed them noisily as far as the police station, where a drowsy askari with a rifle came rapidly to life and waved the children away. Nearby, underneath a large fig tree, a stray dog was sniffing at the limp body of a glossy ibis lying in the dust. Its head was covered in flies. Nobody took any notice.

"The Waterbuck is up there," said Bryony, pointing to a road off the square. They dodged a pair of nuns from the hospital coming out of the post office and arrived back at the car.

"Is that it?" said Max. "The full extent of Nawiri?" An elderly woman walked past the car bent double under an enormous bundle of wood.

"More or less. We passed the church on the way in. The Mission school was behind it."

"Was?"

"It was burned down before Christmas. The teachers wouldn't take the oath, apparently."

"What happened to them?"

"Killed, of course. There's a shady spot by the goods yard near the station. No one will see us there. But we'll have to be quick. Jump in. I promised to be back in time for tea."

4

The following day, Meryl Bottomley walked into the Safari Bar of the Waterbuck Hotel and looked round. John, the bar man, was washing glasses while a hotel boy cleaned out the ashtrays on the bamboo tables. "There's nobody here," she said loudly.

"We are here, Memsahib," said John.

Meryl ignored him and walked out. Five minutes later she returned with her husband, Reginald, and another couple, friends up from Umtali, Southern Rhodesia.

"Four Tusker," shouted Reginald in the general direction of John.

"Yes, Bwana."

While the four installed themselves at a table by the window, John surreptitiously relieved himself into a glass behind the bar. He tipped a quantity of the amber nectar into four clean glasses and topped them up with Tusker lager. He put the glasses and the four half-empty bottles on a tray and took them over to the disagreeable quartet. A curt nod from one of the Rhodesians passed for thanks. John went back to the bar.

"That's better," said Reginald, lowering his glass with a crash. He wiped his mouth on the back of his large, hairy hand. "Have you seen the Big Five yet?"

"The Big Five?"

"Lion, elephant, buffalo, rhino and…"

"Giraffe?"

"No."

"Zebra?"

"No." Reginald was becoming agitated.

"Baboon?"

"No." Reginald was losing patience.

"Cheetah?"

"No," roared Reginald, his face an appalling shade of puce.

"Leopard," said Meryl calmly.

"That's it. Well done, that woman. Four more Tusker!"

"It's the likes of Friend Bumley that give the Europeans a bad name," said James, sitting in his office next to the bar. Max was looking out of the window at a pair of crowned cranes posing on the lawn.

"Perhaps he'll have an accident," said Max. "Charged by a rhino or stuck in the mud, irretrievably."

"Nice idea. Come and have a look at these."

James took Max through the hotel's annual balance sheets for the last ten years. Assets and liabilities, debtors and creditors. Furniture, cutlery, crockery and glassware, linen and bedding…Max's head began to spin. Columns of figures swirled before his eyes.

"In the early years there were no dividends for shareholders. The profits were ploughed back into the business. We started with six bedrooms and now we have fifty-five, each with their own bathroom and…"

"Bwana, come quick. There is a great flood in number thirty-eight. The basin is overflowing."

James rushed down the corridor with the hotel boy and turned off the stopcock. He called for mop and bucket and summoned the plumber to change the washer on the offending tap.

"Never a dull moment," he said, squelching back into the office. "How about a stint with Martha at reception to see how the bookings work?"

On the hotel terrace a group from the Kenya Farmers' Association were in animated discussion about pyrethrum and passion fruit. Mount Kenya was visible in the distance. A haggard man in a stained safari jacket shambled over, pulled up a wooden chair and put his gun underneath it.

"I've just come from the Logans. Mau Mau got their cattle last night. Disembowelled some and hamstrung others. Andrew was away but Margaret shot a couple of the gang as they were running off into the forest."

"Good for her. Is she all right?"

"Putting a brave face on it. The dogs kept them away from the house."

"What about the servants?"

"Made themselves scarce. Looked pretty sheepish this morning, I thought."

"These attacks. They're so random. There's no pattern to them. You never know when or where the next one will be."

Max was looking over the small aviary in the hotel gardens while the birds were being fed. An amiable turaco, violet, green and crimson, landed on his arm and took some food from his hand.

"He likes you, Bwana Max," said Daniel, dipping deep into his galvanised bucket.

"He's very tame. I expect he does this to all the guests."

"Not all. He does not like Americans or Bwana Bottomley."

"What an intelligent bird."

Evidently pleased by the compliment, the turaco bounced onto Max's shoulder and nuzzled his ear before flying to a branch in his cage.

"Where is Memsahib?" said Daniel.

"There is no Memsahib."

"I saw you in Nawiri with a lady. She looked very friendly."

5

Max was lounging in the sitting room at Xanadu a couple of weeks later. He was waiting for breakfast. He did not attempt to emulate James' early start and it did not seem to be expected. He stretched over to a side table and picked up a copy of *The East African Standard*. It was a few days old, but no matter. He was only filling in time. He glanced at various gloomy pieces about the Emergency. A police informer hacked to death in front of his children in a village a few miles south of Nawiri. Four more terrorists hanged in Nairobi. A group of fighters captured in the Aberdares. Much the same as usual.

Max got up and looked out of the window. It was still misty. No sign of Molly yet. She was usually much in evidence at this hour. He wandered towards the kitchen. He could hear Edward and Joseph talking in low, gently modulated tones. When they saw him they stopped. He asked if they had seen Molly.

"Memsahib went out," said Joseph. "She will be back soon."

The slamming of a car door signalled Molly's return. She marched in with a shopping basket and made straight for the kitchen.

"I had to get some more eggs," she said to Max in the dining room. Joseph had brought coffee. "I thought we had plenty but they seem to have vanished. That's not the first time food has walked. It's happened at the hotel too. I'm beginning to wonder if it's finding its way to terrorists in the forests." Molly picked up her bag and checked the small revolver nestling inside. "The servants profess complete ignorance, of course. It's pretty unnerving when you've lived side-by-side with them for years. You don't know who to trust anymore."

"We still have food rationing back home. That's one thing you don't have to worry about."

"You're not homesick?"

"No. England seems very dull and drab in comparison. You never know what's going to happen here."

"That's what worries me, all of us, just at the moment."

Max enjoyed the edge, the sense of danger, but did not say so. There was something stimulating about the undercurrent of unease. Joseph replenished the coffee, put boiled eggs and toast on the table and left the room. Molly nipped out to find a copy of *Country Life*.

The eggs were hot. Max tried to hold his egg steady to remove the top. He burnt his finger and thumb. In a flash of anger and pain he grabbed a knife and slashed at the egg again and again. Yolk, white and shell were spattered over the table. He sat back, panting, exhausted. It had been a while since he had lost control like that, erupted without warning.

He was wiping the table with his napkin when Molly came back with the magazine.

"I'm sorry," he said. "I had a slight accident."

"Not to worry. Joseph will clean it up." She opened the magazine and flicked through it. "I see that Lucy Grendon-Smith is engaged. Pretty girl. We used to know her people in Wiltshire."

6

It was Saturday afternoon. Max was nearing the squash court, housed in a simple box-like structure in the shade of a large fig tree, a little way from the main buildings of the hotel. Two breathless and sweating figures emerged from the court, holding rackets and empty glasses. He recognised the larger man as Reginald Bottomley. He did not know the other.

"Are we still on for tonight, Reggie?"

"Try stopping us." Reginald took the end of the grubby towel round his neck and dragged it across his bright pink face. "We're meeting at Dick's place after the film show at the Club. It should be good fun."

"Are you sure the new district officer's on side? We don't want to be troubled by formalities."

"Absolutely. I've briefed Gamble about the aims of the Association. He understands the need for a little settler justice to help tackle Mau Mau. Turns out we were at the same school."

The other man faltered as he saw Max approaching.

"Don't worry about him," said Reggie. "He's not been here long but I think I can safely say he's one of us." He turned towards Max and said to him, "Hello, old boy. Meet Frank Ellerton. He farms over at Kilmani. Come and join us for a drink."

Max did so with some reluctance but he knew better than to offend a regular customer of the Waterbuck. They sat on the terrace, well out of earshot of the bar. Reggie leaned towards him. The stench of sweat was overpowering.

"We have a little group – commandoes, if you like – who believe that rather more needs to be done in the fight against the terrorist. We call ourselves the Nawiri District Defence Association. I gather you can handle a gun. Do you fancy bagging a few Kukes tonight? No game licence required, ha! There's a bottle of scotch for the highest score."

Max found the prospect both appalling and attractive but he was committed to bridge at Xanadu.

"Perhaps another time. I'm afraid I'm tied up this evening."

"Certainly, old boy. We'll be active for a while yet, I don't doubt. It's all hands to the pump. Frank's brother, Jim, is screening officer at the Kilmani centre."

Frank looked uncomfortable.

"Nothing like a bit of the third degree to encourage Mau Mau suspects to spill the beans," said Reginald, draining his glass and banging it down on the table. "Some of Jim's chaps get a trifle carried away but that's par for the course. We're fighting for survival."

"I think it's time we were off, Reggie."

"Nonsense. I need another Tusker. Boy!"

7

Max was sitting at the piano in the corner of the restaurant at the Waterbuck. He was alone and it was quiet. Breakfast had long been cleared away and the tables set for lunch. In the middle of each table was a small vase of flowers from the hotel gardens. Through the window he could see a pair of rock hyraxes, like giant guinea pigs, sunbathing on top of a wall. He lifted the lid of the piano, put his hands on the keys and shut his eyes. For a long time he did not move. Then he started to play. *Für Elise*. Slowly at first, then faster, and finally slowly again. The last time he had played that had been at Brockley. The baby grand piano in the Morning Room. It seemed a world away.

His mother had always liked it. So had Helga, years before. That summer, over from Austria in the school holidays to improve her English. She used to call it *Für Helga*, sat on the stool next to him, half on and half off. 'Play *Für Helga*, Max.' He did, until the day she got too close. Why did she have to get so close? The memories, and the sensations, came flooding back. She had hardly screamed at all.

Max smiled at the recollection. He did not notice Bryony standing at the doorway. She sensed that it was wiser not to disturb him, to wait till he had finished playing.

"I heard music," she said after a few moments. "I didn't know it was you. You never said you played."

"No."

"You play well."

"Thank you."

"Do you know anything that isn't classical?"

"Such as?"

"I don't know. Noel Coward? Cole Porter?"

Max started playing.

"Do it again."

Bryony began to sing 'Just One of Those Things', softly but with a quiet assurance.

"And you sing well," said Max. "How do you know it?"

"We've got piles of records up at the farm. Absolutely heaps. You must come and listen to them."

James put his head round the door. "I've dealt with the roofing contractors. Can we have a word about the window frames in the new block. When you have a moment."

"It's all right; I'm just going," said Bryony. To Max, she added, "I'll pick you up tomorrow morning. Sorry it's such an early start. It's going to be a long day."

8

The smooth surface of the lake was as blue as the sky. As Max and Bryony walked through the thorn trees to the water's edge, they heard the harsh cry of a Goliath heron disturbed in the feathery papyrus. A lone cormorant stood with outstretched wings on the branch of a dead tree projecting from the lake. Max shielded his eyes and looked back the way they had come, back towards Mount Longonot and the dark bulk of the Aberdares.

"Didn't I tell you it was beautiful here?" said Bryony, making towards a small jetty. A rowing boat, green on the outside and cream on the inside, was tied to a rusty ring at the end. "Let's get in."

"Are we supposed to?" said Max. "It must belong to someone."

"Who cares? We'll bring it back."

The boat rocked gently as they got in. Max put the oars in the rowlocks and untied the painter.

"I haven't rowed on a lake since last summer at Brockley."

"You have a lake?"

"It's not very big, all things considered. Not compared to Lake Naivasha. One of my ancestors dammed the local river. We had a boat house until the roof caved in and sank the punt."

He rowed round an expanse of water lilies while Bryony trailed her hand lazily in the water. A hippo grunted from somewhere close but did not appear.

> *"The Owl and the Pussy-Cat went to sea*
> *In a beautiful pea-green boat,*
> *They took some honey, and plenty of money,*
> *Wrapped up in a hundred bob note.*

What I don't understand," she said, "is why you left a country estate in England to come to Kenya at a time like this."

"It's only for a few months. And it's a lot warmer here."

"You said you were in Aden. That must have been pretty hot."

"That was National Service. This is more of a holiday. Well, working holiday. James had me slaving in the kitchens yesterday afternoon alongside the cooks. 'Important to learn the ropes, old boy. And to see what the staff get up to.'"

When they reached the island in the lake, Max pulled onto a muddy beach. They both leaped out, alarming a flock of pelicans, which rose rapidly in a large white cloud. It was the only one in the sky. He dragged the boat further up the beach and tied it loosely to a tree stump. They walked for some way through an area of short, thick grass dotted with thorn trees. A few antelope grazed with unconcern in the middle distance. Max removed a towel from his bag and laid it on the ground.

"E A R and H." Bryony read out the letters embroidered on the towel.

"East African Railways and Harbours. I got it on the train from Mombasa. A modest souvenir. Well, I'd had to pay extra for the bedding and my de-luxe mattress."

"I'm not sure I should sit on stolen property."

"You weren't worried about sitting in the boat."

"We're just borrowing it. What else have you got in that bag?"

"Bananas and passion fruit from the market in Nawiri. One bottle of water. One knife. One camera. And this."

He took out a revolver and pointed it at Bryony. His finger touched the trigger.

"Is that thing loaded?"

"I suppose it is. Not much use in a hurry without bullets."

"Well put it down, for heaven's sake."

"Don't worry. The safety catch is on. Passion fruit?"

With some difficulty, Max cut the wizened fruit in half and handed the two pieces carefully to Bryony. She extracted the slimy orange flesh with much slurping and tossed the empty shells into the grass. He wetted his handkerchief from the water bottle to wipe the stray pips from her face. A sudden glint caught his eye. It came from the other side of the island. His body went taut.

"We're being watched." There was an urgency in his voice. "Someone's looking at us through binoculars, spying on us."

"More likely looking at birds. The trees over there are full of egrets."

"I don't like being watched. Let's go somewhere less exposed."

There was a look of unease on Bryony's face but it soon passed.

There was no sign of anyone when they returned the boat to the jetty. Bryony sat at the wheel of the car she had borrowed from her aunt, Alison Fox, while Max consumed a banana and threw the skin out of the window.

"Let's go up to Nakuru," she said. "We can have a quick look at the lake and get some lunch at the Boar's Head. We can come back via Thomson's Falls."

By the time they reached Lake Nakuru the sky was grey and overcast. She turned left off the main road onto a track.

"This will take us round the other side of the lake and into the town."

After a while the sky darkened to slate and it began

to rain. Light drizzle became a torrential downpour. The rough, dry track turned to mud, punctuated by deep puddles as the potholes filled rapidly. Bryony negotiated her way slowly. Suddenly, the car slid to a juddering halt. It was stuck fast. The back wheels spun uselessly, gripping nothing.

"Have you got the spade and rope in the boot?" said Max.

"No," she said, miserably. "They're in the other car. What are we going to do?"

He took the knife from his bag and got out of the car. In the driving rain he hacked at the branches of the nearest tree. He pushed a handful of twigs under one of the rear wheels and encouraged her to inch the car forward. The tyre began to grip the twigs. The car shot ahead and was stuck again.

Max, soaked to the skin, swore loudly and kicked the wheel. Bryony looked even more despondent. He cast around for something more substantial. A few yards further on a thin wooden board, bearing the remnants of a poster, dangled by a wire from a concrete post. He yanked the board free, broke it in half over his knee and pushed both halves firmly under the wheel. This time it worked.

He got back in the car and wiped his face and hands on the towel. Bryony put on the headlights and set off cautiously. The windscreen wipers wiped at a manic pace. To left and right, pairs of eyes shone in the semi-darkness. The wild, gull-like cry of a fish eagle came from the other side of the lake. Something crashed out of the bushes behind the car. Bryony stopped and shivered.

"Max. Could you take over until the hotel? It can't be far now."

He settled into the driver's seat. His sodden trousers clung to his legs. He put the car into gear and sped through the gloom. His hands gripped the steering wheel. He was going too fast to avoid the goose on the track. It struck the car with a dull thud. He did not stop. He had a wild, intense look that Bryony found frightening.

"Good God," said Roger Lewis in the lobby of the Boar's Head as two wet and dirty figures came in. "What happened to you? We'd better get you cleaned up."

"Any chance of some lunch?" said Max. "We're starving."

"They've stopped serving but I'll see what they can do."

It was late when they got back to the farmhouse at Naro Moru. The house was in darkness. Alison and Peter Fox were spending the night with friends in Nairobi. Bryony locked the front door behind her, checked the other doors and windows and joined Max in the sitting room. There was no sign of the servants.

"Do you want a drink before I take you back to the pleasure dome? The phone's over there if you want to tell Molly and James where you are. We were due back ages ago."

Max picked up the phone. "The line's dead," he said. "Must be the rain."

Bryony brought him a whisky and soda and had one herself.

"Let's get the fire started. I don't know what has happened to Sammy."

Max retrieved his bag from the chair by the phone and removed the revolver.

"Where's yours?"

"I must have left it in the car. It was in the glove compartment. There's another one in the desk drawer in the study. The key is in the *Complete Works of Shakespeare* in the bookcase."

The fire was beginning to burn when he came back with the gun. Bryony put 'Stormy Weather' on the gramophone and sat with him on the settee. A pleasant drowsiness was beginning to come over her when there was a tremendous crash and shattering of glass. Max leapt to his feet. A man burst into the sitting room wielding a panga. He had long matted hair and wild bloodshot eyes. As he rushed forward Max fired at point blank range. The man fell to the floor, dropping his panga with a clatter on the parquet. Three or four other men following closely behind him turned to run off. Bryony and Max fired in quick succession and hit their targets. Max gave chase and shot blindly into the darkness outside the kitchen window.

He went back to the sitting room, stepping over the bodies lying crumpled on the floor.

"One of those men was Sammy," said Bryony. She was white and shaking. "He got away. We shan't see him again."

Max picked up the pangas strewn on the floor and laid them on the table. A sudden noise made him turn round.

"Don't shoot, it's…"

She was too late. The old cook, Nathan, was blown back by the force of the bullet that hit him. He was unarmed.

Max felt excited, exhilarated by the turn of events. He put his arms round Bryony, who was sobbing gently on the settee. He held her tight, then tighter, then tighter still. She could hardly breathe.

9

The District Police Chief and his sergeant said their farewells and went down the steps of Xanadu. Their dusty Land Rover bumped along the track to Nawiri. The sky was a faint powder blue. Here and there a patch of dampness gave a hint of the downpour of the previous day. A dented car, caked in mud, was parked roughly in the drive.

"Alison and Peter are somewhere between Nairobi and Naro Moru," said James. "The police are going to try and intercept them before they get back to the farm. Do you want a brandy, Max? I know it's a bit early."

He shook his head and stared at the rug on the floor.

"She was such a nice girl," said Molly. "With her whole life ahead of her. Bryony was like a daughter to them. They couldn't, you know."

"The police say she managed to get one of the gang first," said James. "Her gun had been fired. There were just too many of them. You did very well, Max."

"It must have been awful. And to see it happen, right in front of you."

"I wasn't quick enough," said Max.

"Jambo, Bwana Max," said Daniel, slowly swinging his bucket of bird food. "You will stay with us, here at the hotel?"

"I should think so. At least, for the time being."

The turaco hopped onto Max's arm and then onto his shoulder.

"He is very happy about that, Bwana Max."

Part Six

The Present

1

The Yellow Room was aptly named. The walls shone yellow-gold in the afternoon sun filtering through the blinds over the windows on the West Front. In the far corner a large bookcase barred the way to the door that once led into the Chinese Bedroom where Miles and Pamela had slept for so many years, close to their sons until both finally went away.

Max put the book he was reading face down on the tripod table by his chair and stood up slowly. He was a tall man with thick, grey hair and a compelling, almost hypnotic, gaze. The passage of time had softened his features but had done nothing to moderate the penetrating stare that had made Jessica uncomfortable when she first saw his photograph.

She noticed the liver-brown marks of age on the back of his right hand as he put it out. His handshake was surprisingly tentative.

"It's good to see you," he said softly, waving her to

sit down. "Neville was right. The resemblance is remarkable. I think you've already guessed, haven't you?"

She nodded. Her mouth was dry and her throat was tight. Neville went out to make some tea in the small kitchen off the other room.

"How did you know the photograph was me?"

She was silent for a moment, then swallowed and shifted in her chair. "I didn't at first. I had no idea who it was until I came to Brockley. I saw the pictures on the piano. It was clear from the guidebook that the boys must be Marcus and Max and that you were the younger one. That's it, really."

Max smiled wistfully. "I gave that photograph to May over fifty years ago. And the brooch too."

Jessica reached into her bag, produced a scuffed red box and opened it.

He took the box and looked at the brooch for a long while without a word, tilting and rolling it gently so that the badger's eye caught the light of the standard lamp behind him. A smile of the faintest benevolence stole across his face. Then he said, "It was my mother's, Lady Pamela's. I'm afraid I stole it from her dressing table. There was rather a stink at the time. Mrs Finch was suspected but there was no proof, of course."

"Mrs Finch. May's mother?"

"That's right. She lived in the village and helped my mother with the cleaning. May's father was caretaker of the Village Hall. May was their only child. She used to come with her mother to the House from time to time. That's when I met her, after I had come back from National Service. It was a brief affair."

Neville returned with the tea and put it on a low table in front of the fireplace.

"I'll be in the usual place if you need me," he said and left the room.

"May had a baby," said Jessica. "My mother. She never said who the father was."

"It was all hushed up. Marriage was out of the question but May wanted to have the baby and keep it. It was impossible for her to stay round here. Being an unmarried mother in those days…and she was under age. So May was sent to stay with her aunt in Suffolk."

"The Finches just went along with all this?"

"It was in their interests to keep it quiet too but they started being difficult…wanting money and so on. There was a showdown and my parents agreed to give them something on condition we didn't hear from them again."

"Sounds like blackmail."

"I suppose it was. My parents had no money, of course. That's when my father sold the pictures – the two Teniers that have just come back to Brockley. Some of the proceeds went to the Finches, the rest was used to send me to Kenya."

"To get you out of the way for a while."

"Exactly. I went to stay with an old family friend. The plan was to fill in time before I went up to St Luke's."

"St Luke's? Marcus went there too. I saw his name on the oars downstairs."

"Quite right. And so did my father and his father before him…all the way back to Sir Matthew. He was the first Baronet."

Jessica hesitated. "I was at St Luke's myself," she said.

"How extraordinary. I forgot they took girls now."

"Women," said Jessica.

The room had a homely feel, she thought, unlike those on display to the public where everything was pushed back, carefully positioned and cordoned off. This room was lived in. A jumble of styles and periods and continents. Carved wooden figures by the Adam fireplace. Fleshy pink soapstone animals on the walnut bureau. Watercolours of bee-eaters by a gilt-framed mirror. A portable television on the revolving bookcase.

"The style police of the Commission wouldn't approve," said Max, following Jessica's gaze. "If it's not Georgian it has to go. These chairs were banished from the Morning Room. I found them dumped on the second floor. The Commission's idea of authenticity is, or at any rate was, to eradicate all traces of anything brought in after the time the House was built. Two hundred and fifty years of history out of the window. Except in the Kitchen. People like ranges and jelly moulds. And Oscar was eventually let back into the Library. That's the polar bear rug."

"They messed up the colour scheme, though."

"Yes," he sniggered. "But I don't think it matters in the least, do you?"

They picked up their cups at the same time, sipped silently for a few moments, then returned cups in unison to vacant saucers.

"You didn't go to St Luke's," she said.

"I decided to stay on in Kenya. I helped run a hotel and eventually became the manager and then the owner. I developed a few sidelines. Wildlife safaris, trips to the coast, partnerships with other hotels. Took people into Uganda and Tanzania too until that became difficult. Still, things did pretty well and a few investments turned out all right. There seemed every reason to stay and no particular reason to come back."

"But your family was here, including your daughter."

"I made a few visits to Brockley over the years. The last time was when my mother died. By then I'd been in Kenya for nearly forty years and was on the verge of retirement. I had begun to think about ending my days in England but probably wouldn't have done anything if the chance of taking over the apartment hadn't come up."

"The Yellow Room wasn't part of it then."

"You *are* well informed. I wanted more space and the Yellow Room had been my bedroom many years ago. I shared it with my brother when we were younger. A suitable donation to the appeal of the day oiled the wheels as far as the Commission was concerned."

"What about May – and Margaret Rose? Didn't you see them when you visited?"

"I couldn't go to Nettlesham. I didn't exist as far as the Finches were concerned. But I got periodic reports over the years from Marcus while I was in Kenya. He went to Suffolk occasionally to keep an eye on things discreetly. I still wanted to know. Then he moved to America with the advertising job and everything dried up. Look."

Max rose creakily, hands on the arms of his chair, and went over to the uppermost of a nest of tables. He handed her a small photograph in a silver frame. It showed a group at what looked like a fairground.

"The middle one is May. The one on the left is her aunt. Mabel Pargeter was her name." He then pointed to a small girl in a pushchair tackling a mound of candyfloss. "That's…your mother."

Jessica held the frame in both hands. How young May looked. What would she have been then? Barely twenty, she supposed; younger than she was now. And her mother: a mass of curls and a wide smile behind the candyfloss. Rather sweet, really.

She tried to blink back the tears, to retain her composure. "I don't understand what you want," she said. "Why break your silence now, after all these years?"

"I wanted to see you properly, after what Neville had said. And it seemed only a matter of time before you found me anyway. Weren't you looking for me too?"

"In a way. But I didn't know you were here. Neville said you went to live abroad. He didn't say you had come back."

"He wanted to speak to me first. Have you told your mother about any of this?"

"No. It was all supposition and I couldn't see where it would lead."

"And now?"

"I'm not sure. It depends whether you want to see her. She *is* your daughter. But she's over fifty herself now and has lived all her life thinking that she has no father. I don't know how she would take to you turning up after half a century of silence. If you met her, then what?"

"That's rather how I felt. It could go well but it could just as easily not. I think this should be our secret, don't you?"

"Neville?"

"He won't say anything."

"How d'you feel, Miss?" said Neville as they walked slowly down the drive.

"Drained."

"Must have been an emotional business."

"Yes, in a restrained sort of way. Very restrained, considering."

"He's not one for showing his feelings. Not as a rule. Will we see you again soon?"

"I don't know. I've got some thinking to do."

She stopped and balanced her bag on the top of the

park fencing to retrieve a tissue. She pulled out a piece of newspaper with it.

"I meant to say. Did you know William Smith?"

"Who?"

She unfolded the cutting and gave it to Neville.

"That was Billy Smith. I knew him. He always did get into trouble."

"Did they ever solve the crime?"

"I don't believe they did, Miss."

2

She arrived at Number One Pomona Court early the following morning. Instead of taking the lift up to the fourth floor, she plodded down the stairs to the gym in the basement, still churned up by the meeting with Max. She had been exhausted when she got back to the flat and fallen asleep in a chair, still clutching an empty pot of yoghurt.

Quarrenden and Cox had corporate membership of the City branch of Power People and many of their staff made use of it. Even at this hour the place was heaving. Her boss, Roger Pearmain, was doing his customary twenty lengths in the pool before work. Barbara Braeburn from Tax was draping herself over a large ball in a room off to the side. The treadmills were occupied by a collection of trainees from Litigation, preparing for the annual hockey match against the rival firm of Carberry Hogg. Jessica herself made her way from the changing room to a rowing machine, one of a group of five in the far corner of the gym. She had been Captain of St Luke's Women's First (and only) Eight but had not been active on the water since she left.

As she got into her stride, she reflected for the umpteenth time on the events of Sunday afternoon. She could not make Max out. His attitude was ambiguous. He displayed a photograph of his daughter in his room but made no attempt to see her. Even if that had been impracticable while he was in Kenya he had been back for years. What had he been doing all that time anyway? Had he ever been married? Were there any other children? He had been warm, friendly, when they met, apparently open, bordering on the conspiratorial at times. Yet there was something too business-like about it. She would have expected more, meeting his granddaughter for the first time. Perhaps she underestimated the difficulties for him. And had she not been pretty restrained herself, meeting the grandfather she did not know she had? At any rate, he was probably right about her mother. What was to be gained by turning up out of the blue after more than half a century?

3

Brockley House and grounds were closed to the public on Mondays. There were still people about, of course. Cleaners, caterers, gardeners, miscellaneous administrators. Max knew he should be grateful to the Commission. Without it the place would have been demolished long ago or turned into a training centre for a bank or insurance company. And yet he still resented people tramping about the family home, wandering mechanically through the rooms, looking but not seeing, rushing around the grounds and dropping litter. But today he had the place largely to himself and he took advantage of it.

He went into the Morning Room and sat on the piano stool. He looked at the large group of photographs on top of the piano and smiled. It was not surprising that no one had noticed anything missing at first. He guessed that Jessica had been the culprit. He admired her nerve – and no real harm had been done. He lifted the lid and played a few notes, apparently at random. The piano needed tuning. He pulled the stool closer and started playing again, calmly and deliberately. Why it was *Für Elise* he did not know. It just came out that way. Slow, then fast, then slow again.

He thought of Helga, her blonde hair and blue eyes. It was hard to believe she was over seventy now, assuming she was still alive at all. She had liked to hear him play, to sit next to him on the piano stool – until it all went wrong. Why did things always go wrong? At least she went back home quietly, without much fuss or inconvenience, and life carried on.

Not like poor Bryony, forever young. She had liked to hear him play too. She had rather a good voice. Who knows how things would have turned out if they had not got stuck in the mud at Lake Nakuru, if she had dropped him back at Xanadu before returning to the farm? Thinking of Bryony used to bring back the excitement, the thrill, as he relived the events of that evening. Now he merely felt tired and old. The years of covering up and running away and pretending had taken their toll.

He looked up at the de Laszlo portrait. The reproduction in the guidebook did not do it justice. Jessica must be roughly the same age as his mother had been when the picture was painted. The emerald ring on Pamela's hand appeared to sparkle. Was her finger pointing at him?

He looked away. He put the lid of the piano down carefully and went into the Marble Hall. A cleaner, dusting the table to the right of the doors to the Saloon, greeted him cheerily as he stepped over the crimson rope and made for the Terrace. He leaned on the balustrade, the pitted surface of the stone pleasingly rough to the touch. The sun was still on the other side of the House but much of the park was bathed in sunlight. The leaves on the trees were beginning to turn, to rust and orange and gold. Where would he be if not here?

He went down the steps and took a path towards the Lake. The grass was still wet from the dew of the night. At the weekend an outdoor concert would be held here, the last of the season, performed by the Easthampton Chamber Orchestra. A Baroque Extravaganza, the leaflet said, with works by Vivaldi, Bach, Telemann, Purcell and Handel. The concert concluded with fireworks over the Lake. He wondered how the ducks would take to them.

He sat on a bench by the water's edge and looked across to a small island from which weeping willows trailed into the Lake. They used to row to the island years ago, he and Marcus, and have picnics there. Sometimes they lit small fires and cooked sausages in a blackened frying-pan removed from the kitchen at The Sett. He sat for a while, gazing into the middle distance, until the high-pitched yelp of a quarrelsome coot, chasing another across the surface, brought him sharply back to the present.

He felt strangely unsettled. He eased himself up and made his way slowly round the Lake until he came to a path taking him towards the Walled Garden. He ducked under the errant rose at the entrance, opened the door with his key, and went inside. It was warm and still and no birds sang. He did not sit on one of the chairs under the apple trees but just stood in the sun with his hands in his pockets.

He had known there was a granddaughter. His, hers, theirs. He had seen her from a distance when she was a teenager and caught a glimpse in the garden of May's cottage as he drove past after the funeral. Not close enough to see properly. He was shaken when he met Jessica yesterday. Her resemblance to his mother was extraordinary. He was glad she had the brooch. It seemed right. But what now? He could not bring himself to face Margaret Rose. He never had liked the name. And there was a husband to contend with: Jessica's father. He might be a problem. Would she tell her mother after all? He thought not but he could not be sure. If she did, things could so easily spiral out of control. His control.

Max lunged at a cane lying on the ground. He lashed out with it wildly, striking a clump of golden rod again and again and again. He collapsed onto one of the chairs, sweating and breathing heavily. He felt better and worse, exhilarated and exhausted. He had not snapped, lost it like that, for a long time. He looked at the golden rod lying broken on the ground. A butterfly flitted into view and landed on a shattered stem. After a few minutes, he stood up. He had decided on one thing, anyway. He would go and see Messrs Dent and Dent, solicitors, of High Street, Easthampton.

4

October. It was half term at the Richard Brinsley Sheridan School. Duncan Westwood looked out of the bedroom window of the north London house he shared with his wife Nicole. She had left a couple of hours earlier for the Regeneration Department of the Borough Council, where she worked. It was a small flat-fronted house, one of a terrace put up in the early nineteenth century to accommodate the upper working classes but now largely occupied by young professional couples. Whether Duncan and Nicole could still be called young was a moot point but neither of them looked or felt their forty years. Nicole professed herself devoid of maternal feelings and said her career came first. So it was just the two of them, as it had been for over ten years now.

The house felt empty and cold. Duncan felt empty and cold. His breath misted the glass of the window as he sighed, half-focusing on the street below. It was damp from the early morning rain, a glistening band of charcoal, pinched by cars parked tightly on both sides. Wheelie bins left haphazardly on the pavement bore silent witness to the dawn passage of the bin men. He saw their bin, '15 Claxton Street' marked clearly on the lid, hard against the wall of number nine. He made a mental note to retrieve it.

The course on Dutch and Flemish painting was going better than he had hoped or feared. Boisterous peasants and stepped gables had struck a chord with pupils who had seen History of Art as a soft option; they seemed genuinely interested. Pity the headmaster had spotted Tracey Knight wearing a pearl earring. It was rather a nice touch.

He turned to the mantelpiece and picked up a postcard. It was a reproduction of a painting by de Laszlo, the same as the one in the Brockley guidebook now resting in a bookcase in the study. He had heard nothing from Jessica. It was nearly two months. No doubt she had had nothing to report. Why should she anyway? He had only met her once, just for a few hours. Perhaps he should have taken the initiative himself but the longer he left it the more difficult it became and if she had been interested she would have been in touch, wouldn't she?

In the kitchen, he slumped at the table with a cup of coffee, strong and black. He picked half-heartedly at a stale croissant. He and Nicole were going nowhere. They had nothing more to say to each other. She was hardly ever there anyway. Jessica, on the other hand, was a breath of fresh air. Extraordinarily attractive too, in a low-key, unostentatious sort of way. A bit guarded at first but you would hardly expect her to welcome a complete stranger with open arms. He had probably talked too much, been a bit too insistent. Still, she had begun to share her thoughts about the Yellow Room and seemed to want him there when she spoke to that Neville Filbert. He was rather flattered. There was a lot more to her, he was sure of that.

He wanted to see her again. And the small question of Nicole? One step at a time. He was only going to suggest a drink.

Duncan went up to the study and opened a desk drawer. He found a business card under a box of paper clips. He closed the drawer, sat down at the desk and prepared to send an e-mail.

5

Jessica was sitting in the Caffè Napoli in MacDougal Street, Greenwich Village. It was just round the corner from the apartment house in Bleeker Street where she was staying with Victoria Chambers. Victoria and Jessica had been trainees together in Pomona Court. Now Victoria was an assistant in the New York office of Quarrenden and Cox.

She marked her place in *The Golden Bowl* with her dog-eared Metrocard, sipped the cappuccino Maria had brought her and stared at the walls. They were covered in framed photographs of stars of stage and screen, some famous, most forgotten. Each picture bore an effusive greeting 'To Maria and Jo' scrawled by the star in question. A chilled display cabinet hummed contentedly on the other side of the room. A pyramid of chocolate-covered strawberries caught her eye. She was tempted. What was it about chocolate that provided solace and consolation? Perhaps it was just greed. She looked away.

It would only spoil her appetite anyway. That evening, she and Victoria were destined for a restaurant on Prince Street with another friend of Victoria's from work. At least it was not far to go.

She was exhausted. She had walked miles, as she had every day she had been in New York, and still she felt she had barely scratched the surface. Perhaps another time. Watching the handball players on the courts by the West 4th Street subway station she had come over feeling faint. She had grabbed hold of the wire fencing to steady herself. She went back to the apartment to lie down, pausing only to look at the programme posted outside the Blue Note where she and Victoria and a couple of other lawyers had had brunch and listened to jazz on Sunday. As she struggled through the heavy double doors of the apartment block with her big brown bags from Bloomingdale's, the janitor sat impassively in his glass booth, his eyes glued to a small screen. He was more interested in the exploits of Yogi Bear than the trials of Jessica Tate.

It was quieter than it had been the previous evening when trucks were unloading barriers to block access to Sixth Avenue before the Halloween Parade. Yesterday afternoon the streets of the Village had thronged with junior witches and wizards, too cheerful and excited to be frightening. The windows and fanlights of sedate row houses sprouted dripping candles and pumpkin lamps with triangular eyes and toothy grins. Monstrous black spiders' webs and spiky broomsticks appeared on the railings outside.

She looked onto the street and saw the disappearing rear view of Bobby – it was unmistakeably him – heading in the direction of Washington Square with his pristine white poodles, Butch and Femme. Bobby, seventy if he was a day with a serious tan and dyed blond hair, had introduced himself when he let her into the garden in the middle of Gramercy Park as he was coming out with his 'babies'. They had different coloured leads. "Blue for a boy and pink for a girl. Have a nice day." She went back to *The Golden Bowl*.

The door juddered open and Victoria burst in with her friend.

"Hi. I'm Melissa."

Long, glossy, black hair flowed onto her shoulders. It had a blue-green sheen like a raven's wing. Jessica put her in her early thirties. Melissa and Victoria ordered iced tea. She had another cappuccino. They talked about New York and London and Quarrenden and Cox. When it was time to pay and move on, Melissa said, "I'll get this." She put a plastic card on the saucer with the check. Jessica saw the name in gold on blue: 'M M P Brockley'.

Melissa Brockley! Could it be the same one? Jessica said in an off-hand way,

"I went to a Brockley House in England not long ago. The family who used to live there were called Brockley too."

"Why, my dad lived there before he moved to the States. He's Marcus Brockley. *Sir* Marcus, for all the good it does. I'm American born and bred, though. Shame the family doesn't have the House any more.

"What does your father do?"

"Dad's been retired a while. He worked in advertising. Madison Avenue and all that stuff. My brother Matt's a Vice President of Bawson Dachs now. That's the ad agency."

Jessica wanted to keep talking but Victoria was looking restless. The three carried on down MacDougal, past row houses of grey, charcoal and plum, across West Houston Street, and left onto Prince Street. The conversation turned to other things but, after they had ordered at La Fourchette and Victoria had gone off in search of a comfort station, Jessica asked Melissa,

"Have you ever been to Brockley?"

"A couple of times, years ago. I don't remember Sir Miles. He was my granddad. He died when I was little. Lady Pamela was a nice old thing. Always doing good works and trying to keep up appearances. Then she died too."

"The last of the Brockleys. At Brockley House, I mean."

"Well, actually not. My dad had a brother – *has* a brother, I should say – called Max. A totally weird guy who lives in the House like a recluse. Spent all his time in Africa and came back to live at Brockley when Pamela died. I've never met him."

"I wonder what he does?"

"No idea. I expect he rises from his coffin at dusk and terrorises the neighbourhood. All I know is that dad says he's loaded."

Victoria came back, sat down and took a large swig of white wine.

"Melissa's parents have a huge house on Long Island," she said. "Right on the beach at East Hampton. It's a great place for parties."

"East Hampton?" Jessica smiled.

"Mel – that's my other brother – lives with them some of the time. He's an artist. He has a studio there and a gallery on Main Street."

"What's it called?"

"Badger Works. Don't ask me why."

The three drifted down Prince Street towards the subway station on Broadway where Melissa was catching the R train back to Brooklyn. She lived in an apartment, owned by her parents, on the top floor of a house in Park Slope.

"I guess you might be interested in this," she said, removing from her ostrich-skin bag a chunky magazine called *Hamptons Now!* On the cover, a minor socialite in a shiny dress took time out from a charity ball to force a smile for the camera. "Let me have it back some time. Thanks for a great evening. And thanks for your card, Jessica. I'll keep in touch."

The magazine fell open at a page marked by a bright pink Post-it. This month's feature in the regular 'Happy Hampton Homes' section was the five-acre waterfront property of discerning owner ex-adman Marcus Brockley and his lovely wife Vanessa. They had first moved to Gotham from England over forty years ago! They liked it so much they stayed!

In the comfort of a nearby bar, Jessica looked at the article while Victoria ordered a couple of beers. It consisted mainly of pictures of the Brockley's Colonial-style mansion, inside and out, supported by text detailing its design history and the provenance of prominent artefacts. One picture showed Marcus standing by himself on steps running down to the water. He looked tanned and relaxed in mid-blue polo shirt and putty chinos. She recognised his father's languid demeanour and patrician good looks. Max, on the other hand, had inherited Lady Pamela's finer features and prominent gaze.

Another picture had Marcus in the foyer with the elegant Vanessa, an older version of Melissa. Their golden retriever, Horace, lay panting at their feet. To the left of the group, apparently projecting from the wall, was a trompe l'oeil shield. It had a coat of arms in which some sort of animal was lurking. The motto was just legible: *Ecce Meles, Ecce Homo.*

6

Brockley House was closed now until the spring. The trees in the park had largely lost their leaves, exposing a wild filigree of branches like insects' wings. Max stood at the top of the stone steps at the front of the House. Through ribbons of mist, apricot in the morning sun, he could make out the squat tower of the church of St Giles crouching beside the road into the village. A footpath led directly to the churchyard through the grounds. He took it. Recent refreshment of the bark chippings made walking on the path a faintly disturbing experience as the surface yielded softly to every step.

A little way past a clump of horse chestnuts a figure loomed in the mist. It stood rigid, unmoving, oddly truncated. Max's heart missed a beat. He was being watched. He did not like to be watched. But the figure stood sightless and unblinking. It was a statue, now fractured and covered in lichen, brought back from Rome in the 1750s by Sir Matthew Brockley.

Max unlocked the door in the wall and went into the churchyard. It was a gloomy place of yews and angular head stones, green with age. Here and there fresh flowers marked the efforts of people who had not forgotten those who lay here. One such was Billy Smith, whose small granite grave was tended by his younger sister, Janet Trent, now settled on a modern housing estate the other side of Easthampton.

Max did not linger in the churchyard. He went into the church. It was as cold as ice. His breath steamed as he held onto the end of a pew to steady himself. He made his way slowly to the back of the church. Set into the rough wall, just above eye level, was a rectangular stone tablet. He read the simple message carved into the stone: 'In memory of Sir Miles Brockley. Born 5 May 1900. Died 26 March 1980.' Beneath those words another inscription had been added more recently: 'And in memory of Lady Pamela Brockley. Born 17 July 1903. Died 6 November 1991.'

He sat down in a pew. His head was in his hands. From a distance the violent movement of his shoulders could have been mistaken for laughter.

He set off early the following morning. It was a fair distance but he knew the way. When he arrived in Woodbury, he parked the car in the place he always did and walked slowly to the café in the Nettlesham Road. The drive had been more tiring than usual. He was a little breathless as he dropped onto a hard wooden chair at the table in the window. It gave him a good view of the shop opposite called Naughty But Nice. The waitress gave him a smile of recognition as she took his order.

He saw Margaret Rose come and go and come back again. It was hit and miss, as always. She might not have been in that day at all. It could have been a wasted journey. That was a risk he was prepared to take. He looked through the café window at the woman in the well-cut trouser suit. She looked efficient, organised, and discreetly prosperous. A successful businesswoman, by all accounts. She took more after May's side than his. He had never really cared much for May. It had not been serious as far as he was concerned, but then what relationship had been?

Margaret Rose was a Finch rather than a Brockley, it seemed to him. Whereas Jessica…a Tate in name only. Margaret Rose, the little girl in the pushchair, was over fifty. He sighed and gripped the edge of the table, shifting in his chair as he tried to get comfortable. He was not going to tell her now, not after all this time. He had decided.

7

Duncan was sitting at his computer in semi-darkness in the study at number fifteen Claxton Street. Electronic whoops and chirrups and crashes were accompanied by flashing lights and occasional expletives. It was his sixth game of pinball in a row. Left flipper...right flipper...the ball ricocheted from side to side and off the bumpers...concentrate, concentrate. Left flipper...the ball went home. The mission was accepted. Three launches left...two...one. That's it. Target training passed. He was promoted to Ensign. He had never got past Lieutenant Commander. How did anyone get to Fleet Admiral? One ball left. Alien Space mission... Xenomorphs destroyed! He was running out of fuel. Quick: increase fuel supply. Bug Hunt mission. Left, left, right. The ball hit the target and shot straight down between the flippers. Game over.

He thumped the desk and hit the keyboard. He sat back exhausted, drained. He played with his whole body, not just his fingers. His shoulders were rigid and his arms ached. Just over seven million. Could be a worse score but could be a lot better. Time to stop. He was bored. Nicole was at the Aphrodite Nail and Beauty Bar, of all places. The weather, when last he had peeked between the curtains, was grey and miserable.

He glanced at the stapled sheets on the desk. He made out the words by the blue light of the screen. Another letter from the headmaster to parents about school uniform. Pupils are ambassadors for the school…eccentricities or extremes of dress will not be tolerated. All staff are expected to understand the policy and to enforce it, he had told them in the Common Room. Lax enforcement was bad for discipline and undermined the policy. What was it this time? Skirt lengths, hoodies, trainers, jewellery, make up. Blah, blah, blah. Same as usual. He tossed the letter back onto the desk. Now what? Another cup of coffee? He could always check his e-mail, again. What's this? One new message. It was from Jessica Tate! He perked up immediately. What was she doing in the office on a Saturday?

They met the following Thursday evening at a bar in the City. It was Nicole's ceramics night. The bar was not the usual one frequented by Q and C people after work but a little way away in Bismuth Street. It was called Tasso. The front of the bar was noisy and crowded. They worked their way through and found a table free at the back. It overlooked a small courtyard in which tall grasses were illuminated from behind and water bubbled uninterruptedly over ghostly white pebbles.

Duncan procured two large glasses of Bourgueil and two packets of cashew nuts and brought them over. The table rocked gently on its cast iron legs. They looked like the base of an old sewing machine.

"Sorry I didn't reply to your e-mail sooner," said Jessica, placing one hand on the table. The marble top was oddly cold to the touch. "I was in New York. I went into the office at the weekend to go through the messages and pick up some papers for a meeting on Monday."

"They work you hard at Quarrendens."

"You do what you need to do to get the job done. That's what they expect and that's what they get. It's not badly paid."

"Even so. What about your social life? There can't be much time for that."

She paused. "No. Not really. I was concentrating on getting through my traineeship but nothing's changed much now that I have."

Duncan did not press the point. The eye of the badger brooch Jessica had put on as she left Pomona Court sparkled in the light of the wasting candle. The brooch did not go with what she was wearing but that was not why it was there. It was a reminder of their one and only previous encounter, a signal that they could pick up where they had left off.

They sipped their wine to use the silence. After a few moments Duncan said,

"No more news on the Brockley front, then?"

"It's all gone quiet." She badly wanted to tell him but she had promised.

"I'm sure that…what's his name?…Neville Filbert… knows more than he's saying. Has your mother been able to help about the Brockley connection?"

"I haven't asked her. I don't see my parents all that often. We don't seem to have much in common anymore."

"But they are your parents." It sounded like a rebuke but she knew he was right.

"I'll see them at Christmas. I always do."

The dying candle bathed her face in warm yellow light. She really was very striking, thought Duncan. Was there no one else in her life? Probably not. He sensed she was lonely. He was going to ask about New York – MoMA, the Met, the Frick. He had never been there. Instead, he said,

"I was thinking of writing a book about animals in art."

"That's a big subject. But hasn't anything been done already? I mean, you'd have thought it would. I'm sure I've seen books about cats and dogs at least."

"I'll have to do some research."

"There must be lots of pictures of people and their pets. And what about horses? Think of all those Stubbs."

"I'll cover everything from Lascaux bulls to Hockney dachshunds."

"And cows pickled in formaldehyde, or whatever it is." Jessica was warming to the theme and relieved to avoid the subject of Brockley for a while. "My grandmother had a reproduction of that Dürer hare. Didn't he do a rhinoceros too?"

"Yes, though he never actually saw one. He made it look armour-plated and borrowed bits of other animals. Still, who was to know? He sold thousands of prints of it."

"What about lions and tigers? I had some Rousseau posters on my wall at St Luke's. Tigers in the jungle. Very fierce. And there was one called *The Snake Charmer*. That had a spoonbill in it."

"I draw the line at spoonbills," he said, a little too loudly. Heads at nearby tables turned.

She burst out laughing and couldn't stop. Her face came alive, her eyes lambent in the candle light. The wine had gone to her head. She had had nothing to eat since the pain au chocolat ten hours earlier.

"I just meant I couldn't do birds in art as well. That's another book."

"Do you have a view about reptiles? Are snakes in or out?"

"I reserve my position. I'm going to the National Gallery on Sunday. Do you want to come?"

Jessica hesitated. She felt comfortable with Duncan and there was not anyone else. Not at the moment. Not for a while, actually.

"Aren't you...? I mean, I sort of assumed..."

"That at my advanced age I must be married. It's all right. She can't come. She'll be at her mother's."

That was not what she had meant, as he well knew.

On the other hand, looking at pictures could not do any harm, could it?

"What time?" she said.

8

In Brockley village, Neville Filbert opened the door of the wardrobe in the back bedroom of Flint Cottage. He felt around below the dresses and coats hanging there long unworn. His hand caught a handle. He lifted out a small suitcase. It was the colour of strong tea. The case was locked. He took it down to the kitchen and put it on the table. He removed his tool-box from the cupboard under the stairs and selected a screwdriver. The lock yielded in no time.

He opened the lid and took out a grubby canvas bag from which he extracted a package. He unwrapped it carefully and examined what was inside. He turned it over slowly in his hands. Still perfect and as bright as the day he had found it in the bag when his father had slipped into the ha-ha. It had been the devil of a job to get him out and help him over to the Grotto. Lucky it had not been broken in the fall. But now, after so many years, it was time for a new owner, if owner he had been. More like keeper or guardian. It was not his to give away any more than it had been his father's in the first place. He had protected it to protect his father's name.

He discarded the yellowed tissue paper and found instead a large sheet of bubble wrap he had been saving for a rainy day. He used the whole piece and held the edges in place with cellotape torn from the roll with his teeth. He needed three hands. Now for a box. A shoe box ought to do — just. He selected the largest from a pile beside the wardrobe. At one end the box had a picture of a woman's shoe in a style that had once been fashionable. The bubble wrap had made the package bulkier but the top of the box fitted snugly.

Jessica was sitting in her office signing a stack of corporate Christmas cards. Compilation of the list of recipients was an annual festive chore, causing aggravation second only to the angst induced by drawing up the list of invitees to the firm's Christmas drinks party. This year's card reproduced a painting by a seven-year-old depicting the arrival of the Three Wise Men, on motorbikes rather than camels. The artist was a pupil at the inner city school to which various Q and C staff went for an hour every fortnight to hear the children read. It was the human face of Quarrenden and Cox. Some called it community involvement or outreach work; others called it *pro bono*. Either way, a few of the older partners were a little uncomfortable at the firm's engagement in noncommercial activity verging on social work and did not shout it abroad.

"It's that man again," said Linda, sticking her head round the door. She was still holding the plastic fork she used to spear her potato salad. "The one who rang before. Neville Filbert. He says do you mind if he has your home address? He wants to send you something."

It was Saturday afternoon. Jessica was curled up with her book, a copy of *The Hours* she had bought at Barnes and Noble on Union Square. Some music was playing quietly in the background. She looked up and saw that it was getting dark. As she stretched to close the curtains she heard the entry phone. The clicking of buttons was followed by a strained and crackled voice.

"It's Filbert here. Can I come up?"

She took Neville's coat and offered him a cup of tea and some Jaffa cakes. He looked worn out. He sat back, pink and panting, with a carrier bag between his knees.

"I'm sorry I'm late. I got lost. I'm not used to London."

"That's all right. Thanks for ringing. Sorry I had my mobile switched off."

"I got your home number from directory inquiries when I decided to come. In the end, I thought it better to bring it rather than send it. It's a bit fragile and you never know with the post, do you?"

"What is it?"

Neville pulled a parcel from his carrier bag and gave it to Jessica with both hands.

"Let's call it a Christmas present," he said.

"Thank you. And you brought it all this way."

A statement of the blindingly obvious. She did not know what else to say. She was thoroughly embarrassed. Should she have got him something? It had never occurred to her. Should she offer to pay his fare? She thought better of it. She looked at the parcel neatly wrapped in holly paper. It was quite light for such a large package. What should she do with it? She remembered the mysterious parcels she had as a child, with jolly Father Christmas labels and stern injunctions not to open until Christmas Day. They were put smartly under the Christmas tree. She did not have one. It did not seem worth it when she lived alone.

"I can take it home with me," she said weakly. "I'm going to my parents for Christmas. It'll be a surprise."

"I shouldn't do that," Neville said quickly. Then more slowly, "It might get damaged on the way. You could open it now. May I suggest you do it at the table?"

She fetched a pair of scissors from a drawer in the kitchen and performed the delicate task of extricating the item from the box. She cut the final piece of cellotape and gently unfurled the bubble wrap. The object inside was gradually becoming clearer. And there it was! She put it in the middle of the table.

"It's beautiful," she said. "But…"

"It's Meissen," said Neville. "Kändler was the man's name. There are a lot more of his pieces at Brockley."

"You don't mean you…"

"No, Miss. I didn't bring this from the House. I've had it in the bottom of a wardrobe for more years than I care to remember."

He told no lies. It was his father who had removed it from Brockley House half a century before. Tom Filbert had coveted the porcelain peacock. He was not supposed to go into the main part of the House but the French windows were often left open. No one saw him go in and stand in front of the cabinet, one of several crammed with porcelain: Meissen, Chelsea, Bow… . Eventually, he succumbed to temptation. It was easy. The cabinet was not even locked. He opened the door, reached for the bird and lifted it out. To fill the gap he moved some of the other figures – a shepherd and shepherdess and a couple of stray members of a monkey orchestra. Then he panicked. He did not know what to do with the peacock. So he wrapped it in a couple of old handkerchiefs and a bit of newspaper and hid it in the walled garden to buy time and to keep it out of harm's way. The Brockleys never noticed it was missing.

Jessica turned the peacock in her hand. It was brilliant turquoise and finely wrought. She looked at the crown and the detail of the tail.

"You said you liked the peacocks when you were down at Brockley. So I thought you might like this."

"I do. It's magnificent. I don't know what to say." She pointed to the tail feathers in the vase on the mantelpiece. "I found those on the grass the first time

I was at Brockley and brought them home. It was a bit awkward on the train."

"The eyes of Argus," said Neville, looking mysterious. "I often explain it to visitors. He was a giant with a hundred eyes, killed by Hermes when he was asleep. Hera took the eyes and put them in the tail of her bird, the peacock. Lorca never liked the peacocks. He was the butler and Lord High Everything Else in Sir Miles' day. He said they watched him with their eyes. Nonsense, of course. Mind you, Mr Max has never liked them either."

"The guidebook said something about a Gypsy's warning years ago that the Brockley family would lose the House if the peacocks came to harm."

"That was long before the war, in Sir Magnus' time. He let the Gypsies camp by the river in Long Meadow, or so my father used to say. Apparently, Sir Magnus had his fortune told one year by Rosa Smith at the Brockley village fair. She mentioned the peacocks. I don't think she meant porcelain ones, though."

9

W hat about insects?" said Jessica in the café at the National Gallery next day. She was wearing one of her new blouses from Bloomingdales. A silver Christmas tree with large pink balls loomed over her left shoulder.

"No room," said Duncan.

"Fish?"

"Ditto."

"Have you decided about reptiles?"

"They're out, along with amphibians."

"You need some animal categories or themes."

"Yes, I…"

"There are domestic animals, like cats and dogs. Farm animals, those used in sports or hunting, and wild animals. Then there are mythological beasts, like dragons and unicorns. I hope they're in."

"Yes, they…"

"Of course, there are overlaps. Some animals could

appear in more than one category. Dogs might be pets or used for hunting. At least, they used to be. Monkeys are wild animals but I've seen pictures of them as pets. There's that one of a girl with a monkey at Brockley, isn't there?"

"Yes, there…"

"The same goes for cheetahs. Then there's bear-baiting…"

"And badger-baiting."

"Oh." She looked crestfallen.

"John Clare wrote a poem called *The Badger*. I came across it in a book the other day. '*The badger grunting on his woodland track/With shaggy hide and sharp nose scrowled with black…*' And so on. The badger gets caught and baited with dogs but he sees them off. I'll lend you the book if you like."

"Yes, please, if the badger's all right. That would be nice. It's a cete, by the way."

"What is?"

"The collective noun for badgers."

"Really? I've never heard of it."

"Nor had I. I found it in on a badger website, would you believe. I don't think the word's used any more."

"Perhaps people don't feel the need to refer to badgers in bulk."

After a pause, she said, "Have you thought what you mean by art? Is it just paintings or other things too?"

"Such as?"

"Sculpture, for example. Or tapestries."

Duncan put his head in his hands. "I'm beginning

to wish I hadn't started this. I may have bitten off more than I can chew. Where will it end?"

"You can't stop now," she said. "It's beginning to get interesting. I'd like to see how things develop."

10

It was six months since May's funeral, six months since Jessica had been back to Suffolk. She woke as the first spark of day lit the eastern sky. She crawled out of bed, had a stealthy shower and slumped at the breakfast bar with a hot cup of coffee and a cold mince pie. She left the house and took the quiet, paling road from Woodbury to Nettlesham. She parked the car by the station.

Her parents had been dead to the world, sleeping off the effects of last night's Boxing Day drinks with the neighbours, fellow-residents of the four-bedroom executive homes clustered in the horseshoe named The Lea after the field built over by one of the various property companies in which Jack Tate had an interest.

"Great house for a party," said a thickset man standing by the enormous plasma screen that dominated one wall of the sitting room. He had a glass of red wine in one hand and a slice of pizza in the other. "And plenty of room if you want to play afterwards, if you know what I mean." Jessica had a pretty good idea. She had seen the thin mattresses piled up in one of the bedrooms, the boxes of miscellaneous products from Naughty But Nice stacked in a corner.

"Have you tried the hot tub?" asked the man's wife, bouncing bralessly towards them. "Canadian red cedar and it seats six."

She shook her head.

"You should. Jack and Margaret invited us over to christen it with a couple of friends last month. You get to know people that way."

The air was cold and crisp as she set off along the estuary, breath steaming in puffs and curls. The light at that hour had an intensity that threw everything into sharp relief, a clarity that would be softened, merged and lost with the progress of the day. The tide was on the rise. Mud flats criss-crossed by the tracks of busying birds were disappearing fast, covered by the lapping waters of the River Nete. The shrill call of oystercatchers flying low echoed from the far shore, quavering at the foot of shadowy pines.

She walked briskly past the silent boat yards, past the lines of upturned dinghies, past the beds of reeds neither shaken nor stirred by the wind but moving gently in unison. Their feathery heads shone silver-grey in the sun. A profusion of craft by the yacht club jetty nodded sedately, ignoring the frantic protests of the seagulls wheeling above. She made her way along the path, greeted by occasional dog-walkers she did not know from Adam. She always forgot that outside London people spoke.

Rounding a bend, she made for the strategically-placed bench three steps down. The spot was warm and still. She took off her matching scarf and gloves and the red beret Duncan had given her and placed them neatly on the bench. Her neck and shoulders ached as she tried to relax and unwind, the back of the bench pleasurably hard all the same. Why did she always feel worse when she stopped?

She had not mentioned Duncan at home. She still called it that. What could she say anyway? And if they knew he was married, only nine years younger than her father. Apparently the rules were different behind closed doors in the recreational world of Naughty But Nice.

"Got yourself a boyfriend yet?"

"You know what they say, Jess. All work and no play."

"Have you tried the internet?"

"We're only thinking of you. We just want you to be happy."

The sun was high in the clear blue sky. The bright light reflected off the corrugated surface of the water hurt her eyes. She put up a hand to shield them. A soggy black Labrador waded through the seaweed at the water's edge, a stick held tightly in its mouth. The dog stopped and looked at her mournfully before ambling off, tail waving gently.

She wondered what Duncan was doing now. He and Nicole had no particular plans, he had said. A few duty visits to relations, perhaps the odd antique fair, and a bit of work on Canaletto for next term. Not long to go.

The days of the week had never mattered much to her before. Monday, Tuesday…it was all the same. She drifted through them and time passed. Now Thursday evenings with Duncan gave the week a fixed point, more of a structure, and gave her something to look forward to. She saw him on most Sundays too.

And yet it was odd to think of him being with someone else, even if that person was his wife. She tried not to resent it; she could hardly complain, after all. He spoke about Nicole rarely, and then more in sorrow than in anger. She obviously did not make him happy, but could she, Jessica, do any better over months and years?

She extricated a book from her tight coat pocket but did not open it. She stared at the ducks quacking expectantly near her feet, the iridescent sheen of the males reminiscent of the peacocks at Brockley and of the porcelain figurine standing proud in the middle of her mantelpiece.

"You've only one life, Jess. Use it well. You won't be able to turn the clock back. Hold out for what you want – but don't leave it too long. You don't want to end up alone. Believe me." Her grandmother's words, quiet advice, imparted in this very spot last summer after potted shrimps and toast at the café on the other side of the estuary. She blew her nose loudly and startled a duck. One corner of the handkerchief was embroidered with the letter 'D'.

Walking back, the trees on her left, mushroom, yellow ochre and purple-brown, winter colours against the flooded fields. A sudden flash of white marked the landing of a solitary egret by a line of contorted willows. Looking towards the town, sliced by the spears and lances of the boats between, the spire of St Edmund's rising above a huddle of red roofs old and new. She stopped to pick up some shells, cockles heaped by the side of the path, before making her way to number twelve Oyster Lane, May's home for many years and now the weekend retreat of a London barrister.

11

Jessica's friend Clare clumped up the stairs to the top floor and pushed at the half-open door of the flat.

"Something's different," said Clare as Jessica took her coat, brushed off the remaining snow and hung it up behind the door. "What is it?"

"Oh, we've just moved a few things around, added some pictures, a few lamps. Not much, really."

"We?"

"Well, me…and Duncan."

"Ah, the elusive Duncan. I was beginning to wonder if he really existed. Has anyone actually met him?"

"He doesn't have much free time. I only see him once or twice a week myself."

"Hm. I thought you weren't getting a tree." Clare was looking at the small Christmas tree in a red plastic pot on a table in the corner. Its lights winked and twinkled periodically.

"Duncan thought I should, even though I was going

home for Christmas. We got it in the market. I should've undecorated it on Twelfth Night but it seemed a shame. I'll see if Sylvia or 'The Boys' want to plant it in the garden."

Clare finished her second crumpet, put the plate on the floor and said, "So he's fifteen years older than you – and married. Are you sure it's…I mean, you don't exactly have his undivided attention, do you?"

"We get on. Talk the same language. He makes me laugh, doesn't let me take myself too seriously. I feel comfortable when I'm with him."

"You certainly seem happier and more relaxed."

"I don't have to put on a performance or make an effort. That means a lot after a day at Q and C being the super-efficient Miss Tate."

"Where's it heading, though? How long do you want to be the Other Woman? They don't leave their wives, most of them."

"I don't know. It suits me at the moment. I don't want to be rushed."

Was Duncan just using her; playing around, a younger woman on the side, to drop when he got bored – or found out? She was as sure as she could be that this was not how it was. Even so. Things could not go on like this forever. Sooner or later he would have to make up his mind. She thought it best not to push him too far too fast. She did not want to lose him. She was sure about that too.

She felt bad about keeping him in the dark about Brockley and Max and meeting Melissa in New York. She had come close to telling him several times. And what could she say when he admired the porcelain peacock the first time he came back to her flat? She just said it was a family piece – which it was, of course.

12

She parked the car outside the house and traipsed up to her flat with bags bulging. She had been to the farmers' market held on the third Sunday of the month at the School of St Martha and St Mary. The severe Victorian pile, rising above the neighbouring terraces, had a large asphalt playground where the stalls were set up. She put olives, stuffed vine leaves and cheese in the fridge alongside the guinea fowl. The walnut loaf, still wrapped in its tissue paper, went in the bread bin and the rest massed on the work surface – apples and pears in one heap, broccoli, parsnips, and potatoes in another. Something was missing.

She ran downstairs to the car and found them on the floor behind the back seat, the vibrant orange tulips she had bought to cheer the place up a bit. It was the first proper meal she had cooked for Duncan. No need to panic, she had hours yet. Nicole was off to a management course at a hotel near Gatwick Airport, away for a whole week! Jessica had already changed the sheets, fished out the new pillows and weathered Edward's reproachful eye as she moved him to the chair by the bedroom window. The Naughty But Nice catalogue slipped easily under the bed.

As she backed slowly out of the car, clutching a bunch of flowers, she heard an irregular but insistent tapping, alternately dull and sharp. Sylvia Beech, making a rare foray from her ground-floor flat, appeared to be striking the cherry tree. Pale-pink blossom floated to the ground.

"It's mild for February, isn't it?" said Sylvia, raising her stick with effort. It had a brass handle in the shape of a duck's head.

"What *are* you doing?" said Jessica.

"It's Boris. He's gone missing. I haven't seen him for two days now."

Jessica saw a photograph of the large black-and-white cat glued roughly to the notice Sylvia was pinning to the tree. She had covered it with polythene cut from an old bag.

"That should do it," she said, as the duck's head went home.

"I hope he comes back soon," said Jessica, taking her gently by the elbow and leading her towards her flat. "I'll let you know if I see him."

"He's all I've got. I'd be lost without him." She negotiated the steps down to her front door, one hand on the rail to the side. "Would you like a cup of tea?"

Sylvia brought two mugs to the table nestling in the

bay window and returned with a packet of biscuits. She brushed a silver-grey hair off the cloth and subsided onto a chair, pulling her cardigan about her.

"I've put your flowers in water. Very colourful. Are they from your young man?"

Jessica coloured. "I bought them this morning."

"But you do have a young man, don't you? I've seen him, both of you, through the window."

"He's not that young, really."

"Well, I'm very pleased anyway. You look much happier when you're with him."

"I…"

"You and that Alastair from upstairs just looked like two singles together. With this one you look like a couple."

"We seem to get on."

"I should say so. Does he have a name?"

"Duncan."

"Like the King of Scotland. I hope yours has better luck. Can I tempt you to a custard cream?"

"Do you know him from work?" The sleeve of Sylvia's cardigan stroked one of the spider plants sprouting from yoghurt pots lined up on the window sill.

"No. He's a teacher, in north London."

"I was a teacher in that part of the world for a while. Years ago. I must have been in my early twenties. I became friendly with the gym master. Ex-army, bit of a rough diamond, but that didn't worry me. I used to see him in the gym after school. We took care to be discreet but one afternoon a boy came back to look for his pumps. He found us *in flagrante*, as they say, and word soon got out. We were out pretty soon too. His wife discovered where I lived. Hurled abuse and sent the most dreadful letters to my landlady, local shopkeepers and the like. I had to move but she pursued me. Eventually I went to Canada, but that's another story. Would you like some more tea?"

Jessica shook her head slowly, wistfully, and went to retrieve the tulips.

13

Dent and Dent occupied comfortable premises in a row of Georgian town houses at the quieter end of Easthampton High Street. But for a small brass plate to the right of the front door, there was no indication that the firm was there at all. The front door was slightly ajar. Jessica shook the March rain from her umbrella onto the greening stone steps and went in. The glass-panelled inner door snapped sharply back into place with a bang as she stumbled into the reception area.

"I've come to see Mr Dent," she said.

The girl sitting behind the vase of daffodils looked up from her magazine. She clearly resented the intrusion.

"Would that be old Mr Dent or young Mr Dent?"

Jessica took the letter from her bag.

"It's Mr P A Dent. I have an appointment."

"That would be old Mr Dent. And you are?"

"Jessica Tate."

"That's right," said the girl, consulting a large black

desk diary. "They're waiting for you. Up the stairs and first door on the left."

They? She knocked and went in without waiting for an answer. The image she had formed of old Mr Dent, pince-nez and white whiskers, was rapidly dispelled by the suntanned man in the charcoal suit and silk shirt who welcomed her and invited her to sit down. His dark brown hair was only slightly greying at the temples. Three chairs were arranged in a semi-circle in front of his desk. Two were already occupied. The occupants had turned round and looked expectant.

"I think you already know Mr Filbert." It was Neville who had told her the news about Max. He had found him slumped on a chair in the Walled Garden. A heart attack, apparently. She was glad that Duncan had been with her when he rang that Thursday evening.

"And this is Mrs Trent." She did not recognise the middle-aged woman in the thick green cardigan and glasses.

An unidentified youth loitering on one side of the office plied them with coffee and shortbread. The stains on his polyester tie could well have been egg. Mr Dent handed round copies of the will and got down to business.

"In plain English, Mr Brockley has left £750,000 to the Heritage Commission, £20,000 to the Brockley Village Hall Fund, £100,000 to you Mr Filbert, £20,000 to you Mrs Trent…"

"Twenty thousand quid? What on earth for?" said Mrs Trent. "I hardly knew him. I'm not complaining, mind. But why?"

"I can't help you, I'm afraid, but Mr Brockley expressly requested that you continue to put flowers on the grave of one William Smith for as long as you are able to do so. It is not an absolute condition as it could not be readily enforced, you understand."

"No, I don't. What's it got to do with Mr Brockley?"

"The will is silent on the matter. If I may continue, certain specified documents and other items are left to Sir Marcus Brockley of Long Island, New York. The balance of the estate goes to you, Miss Tate."

"To me? But…"

"It's too soon to say exactly how much it will be. There will be various amounts to deduct – inheritance tax, outstanding debts and sundry expenses, that sort of thing – but I think I can safely say that it is a not altogether insubstantial sum."

A little later, when the others had left the room, Jessica put the question.

"I can't commit myself at this stage," said Mr Dent, "but I should think we're talking about something between three and four million pounds."

That afternoon, she sat in an armchair at Flint Cottage nursing a mug of tea. She was staring at the patterns in the rug in front of the fire.

"It's ridiculous," she said. "I only met him once. You knew him far better."

"Far longer, anyway," said Neville. "He always was

rather secretive. I think he wanted to keep things in the family."

"What about Marcus? Surely Max should have left his money to him?"

"I don't think Sir Marcus is short of a bob or two, if I may say so."

And what about Margaret Rose? "Max must have changed his will," she said. "Someone's going to ask who I am and why he left his estate to me. If they haven't already." She was thinking of Mrs Trent. And surely Marcus' side of the family would not let matters lie? "Is Marcus coming to the funeral?"

"He said he would, Miss. He may bring his daughter with him."

Jessica looked at the embers glowing in the hearth. The prospect of being a millionaire filled her with gloom. All she could see were the problems. How would she explain her sudden wealth and what would she do with it?

"You could always say you won the lottery," said Neville. "Or just keep quiet about it. By the way, I've been keeping this for you. Max wanted me to look after it, just in case." He stretched and retrieved the envelope from the mantelpiece. She opened it. There were two photographs inside. Both showed Jessica with her mother walking along a path above some mudflats. Small boats lay on their side, waiting for the tide to set them free. The photographs looked as though they had been taken about ten years earlier.

"How did he get these?"

"I think he must have taken them himself."

"So he knew about me all the time?"

"I don't know how long he knew but it was your turning up at Brockley that changed everything. I think it affected him more than he let on."

"That'll teach me to look in other people's bedside cabinets," she said, wiping her eyes on the large white handkerchief that Neville had produced with a flourish. Right on cue, as always.

14

They were sitting in the park opposite her flat on the following Sunday afternoon. Nicole, it seemed, was no more at her mother's that day than she had been on any of the other Sundays that Jessica and Duncan had been together. Officially, he was doing some research on representations of animals in wartime. Nicole was not likely to check, he assured Jessica; she had no interest in art anyway.

The trees were gaunt and leafless but here and there were signs of life, the beginnings of buds, a hint of more to come. The rough grass, speckled with worm casts and the droppings of Canada geese, had yet to have its first cut of the year. The sky ran the gamut from pewter to eau de nil. An unkempt forsythia blazed between their bench and the privet hedge beyond.

"It's an ambiguous colour, yellow," said Duncan. "It signals birth and renewal in spring, and death and decay in autumn. You don't know where you are with it."

"It's a warm, cheerful colour," said Jessica. "Like the sun is – or would be if we could see it."

"It's an unhealthy colour too. Makes me think of illness. Yellow fever, jaundice. No wonder quarantine flags on ships were yellow."

"Bananas and custard?"

"Lemons and grapefruit – sharp and citric."

"Butter... and mango sorbet."

"Brimstone, sulphur. Like the fires of Hell." He sounded suitably diabolical.

A light drizzle dowsed the flames. It came on to rain harder. They hurried to take shelter in the empty bandstand, a dismal octagon much abused by dogs and local youth. The rain bounced through the open railings and wet the floor.

"Your hands are cold," said Duncan.

"Yours aren't. You know what they say: 'Warm hands, cold heart'. He looked hurt, but not very. "Of course, there are exceptions to every rule." She kissed him gently on the lips.

It had been a relief to tell him. With Max dead, she felt under no obligation to keep the promise she had made. His death had removed a barrier, brought her and Duncan closer. She told him about meeting Max and Melissa, and showed him the photocopy of the *Hamptons Now!* article that Victoria had taken for her. Then she mentioned the money coming her way when everything was settled. He looked downcast and said he hoped it would make no difference, to them. "No.

Of course not. Why should it?" But it might help to concentrate his mind, she thought. Overcome any financial barriers to his leaving Nicole. Not that she had any idea what to do with the money but she had no plans to do anything rash, like throwing in her job with Quarrenden and Cox. And her parents? Best to keep quiet, Duncan agreed.

It was odd to think that Max had known about her all the time, watched her and her mother from a distance. More than odd. Disturbing. How many times had Max been there over the years looking, spying, taking pictures? The thought was unsettling but it had surely been worse for him, always on the outside, quietly observing the daughter and granddaughter who never knew he existed. He could not bring himself to meet them but he could not stay away.

It was still raining when the sun came out, a curious light that bathed the park in copper-yellow and brought it back to life.

"Look. There's a rainbow," she said, pointing to the arc that appeared to end between the tower blocks in the distance. "Richard Of York Gained Battles In Vain. All present and correct. The York's not so bad, is it?"

"Not when it's surrounded by the rest of the spectrum. It becomes a different colour."

"I don't know why they talk about a peacock's feathers being 'iridescent'. They don't look much like a rainbow."

"I think it's because the colours change in the light, or seem to."

"Tea?"

As they were leaving the park, she turned Duncan towards a large patch of flowers by the gate.

"What's supposed to be wrong with those daffodils?"

They were narcissi but he took the point.

15

After the funeral at St Giles', Marcus came up to her and said, "I guess you must be Jessica."

Neville hovered at a distance, calm, impassive, a reassuring grey eminence. Marcus was a tall distinguished-looking man with all his wits about him. It was odd seeing him in the flesh after all this time. He seemed less relaxed, more on ceremony, than in the magazine pictures. Perhaps that was not surprising. He had travelled from New York alone and was staying at a hotel off Piccadilly. Neville had picked him up from the station.

"Max was right. You do look just like our mother, Lady Pamela."

"So people tell me. I can never see it myself."

"She was a beautiful woman in her day."

Jessica blushed. As they walked towards the House, she said, "So you knew all about me too."

"I wouldn't say that. But I've had reports, on and

off, over the years. Reports of sightings, mostly. Views from a distance. Max liked to watch."

"And then he met me."

"Yes. I guess he was pretty apprehensive about the prospect of meeting you but glad he did. It rounded things off, in a way."

"We only met once."

"It was enough. For him, I mean. That's all he needed. Max never was much good at longer-term relationships. He was too volatile; things always went wrong."

In the Marble Hall trestle tables with white cloths were laden with food and drink.

"I believe they call it a finger buffet," said Neville, juggling plate and glass as he bit into a samosa. "They've catered for a lot of fingers."

"There are a lot of people here," said Jessica. The sounds bounced off the hard surfaces of the Hall, making it increasingly difficult to hear. "I suppose I'd better mingle."

She wove around knots of men in suits and huddles of women in hats, wondering who they all were and how far back they went. Did they know or care that Max had left most of his money to her? She turned heel at sight of Mrs Trent loitering by a fireplace making short work of something on a stick. She did not want a re-run of the meeting at Dent and Dent.

She sank onto a small hard chair next to a woman with iron-grey shoulder-length hair. The woman was removing a fugitive piece of egg mayonnaise from her blouse with the corner of a paper napkin. The job done and introductions made, Jessica asked, "What's your connection with Max?"

"I first knew him in Kenya. She still pronounced it 'Keenya', unlike Max. I was called Susan Campbell-Hill then. He stayed with my parents. They ran a hotel and eventually he did too. It was a difficult time during the Emergency. My late sister, Jennifer, and I spent part of the time in England."

"What was he like in those days?"

"Charming, in many ways. Popular with women but I'm not sure he liked them. Another woman was just another tick, or so it seemed, like twitchers and their birds. Not that he tried anything with us. Too close to home, I suppose. He couldn't have walked away so easily."

"He was there a long time."

"Yes. But I don't think he really settled even when he stayed, if you see what I mean. There was always an odd sense of detachment, as if he wouldn't or couldn't engage. I can't quite put my finger on it."

"You said you *first* knew him in Kenya," said Jessica, relieving a passing waiter of a brace of goujons.

"I came to live in England for good donkeys' years ago. I met him again at Pamela's funeral and he said he was thinking of coming back. I saw him a few times after he did."

"Had he changed much?"

"Mellowed," she said slowly. "Yes, mellowed."

"I wonder how he spent his days."

"He said he was going to write his memoirs, said

he had things to get off his chest. I'm not sure what. Looks like he never did, anyway."

Suddenly, the cry went up. "*Toro! Toro!*"

Neville hurried by. "My sisters," he said, as if in explanation. He went to join the delighted women by a chair near the front door. It was occupied by a new arrival, an elderly white-haired man of vaguely Latin appearance. As he greeted Neville warmly, the man looked over his shoulder and stared at Jessica on the other side of the Hall.

"Ees not possible," he said. "Ees Lady Brockley." He looked as though he had seen a ghost.

Neville turned and beckoned to her. "This is Lorca," he said. "He used to work here, many years ago."

It was mid-afternoon. The Hall was nearly empty now. Marcus emerged from the Saloon and joined Jessica for a cup of tea.

"I've been looking at the pictures in the Red Drawing Room," he said. "It's good to see those Teniers again after all this time. I used to stand and stare at them for hours. The more I looked, the more I saw. I was pretty upset when I heard they'd gone. It seemed like a part of my childhood had gone with them."

"Max told me why they were sold."

"Did he also tell you how they came back?"

"No. The papers just said the Commission bought them with the help of an anonymous donor."

"Max tracked them down years ago but the owner refused to sell. Then she died and the family were persuaded to part with them. The Commission fronted the transaction but most of the money was provided by Max. I guess he felt guilty the pictures were sold in the first place."

Marcus put his empty cup and saucer down with a clink and said, "I thought I might take a look at the Yellow Room while I was here." No more was necessary or forthcoming.

He unlocked the door marked PRIVATE at the top of the stairs with the key Neville had lent him. As they pushed through the inner door to the room on the right Marcus said nothing for a while. He raised the blinds of the windows overlooking the West Terrace and the grounds beyond. A weak sun came out from behind a cloud. The room was not the golden-yellow that Jessica remembered from the day she had met Max six months before but a pallid, sickly colour.

"Yellow," said Marcus. "The colour of cowardice. Max always did run away."

"Wasn't it your room as well at one time? You went away too. At least Max came back, eventually. Sorry, I…" But she had felt the need to defend him.

"I had a job to go to. I didn't run," he said sharply. Then he added in a softer tone, "Well, maybe I did, in a way. From my responsibilities here as the next in line. I felt I was being groomed to take over almost as soon as I could walk. It was a losing battle, though, trying to keep this place going. Seeing my parents struggle, I wanted nothing to do with it. There was no future in it. I was part of a different world by then. But, as you say, it was Max who came back when my mother died and kept a Brockley living in the House."

"What will happen now?"

"Max will be the last, unless…"

"No. I'm not a Brockley anyway."

"Maybe not in name but you are Max's granddaughter – and my great-niece, too. Not that it feels like that, despite my advanced age. You're not much younger than Melissa. I guess the generations have got out of synch."

Marcus moved over to the nest of tables near the fireplace and picked up a small photograph in a silver frame. "I took that fifty years ago at the fair in Nettlesham," he said, "and sent it to Max in Kenya. I must have been about your age then." He stared at the small girl sitting in a pushchair with an enormous mound of candyfloss.

"There's someone in Suffolk I'd like to see before I go back," he said. "Would you care to come with me?"

Epilogue

The Present

Are you sure you want to go through with this?" said Duncan in the subterranean café in a street off Leicester Square. A pile of sugar lumps lay on the table between them.

"He was rather persuasive," said Jessica. "It seemed important to him."

"But pretty awkward for you. I thought we'd agreed you'd keep quiet. He can just fly back to New York leaving you to clear up the mess."

"I know. But if he meets my mother the secret's out whether I'm with him or not. Besides…"

"What?"

"I was wondering about going to New York too and seeing the rest of my new family. He hasn't told Melissa yet and I didn't like to when she e-mailed to tell me Max had died. It seemed better coming from her father than from me."

"How long will you be away?"

"I meant us, not just me."

"Both of us?"

"Yes. I'd like you to be with me."

"It'll have to be in the school holidays."

"What will you tell Nicole?"

"I don't know. I could always say it was research for the book."

"Suppose she wanted to go with you? Do some shopping while you beavered away?"

"I'll have to play it by ear. She may not want to go at all."

And if she does, thought Jessica? Maybe the time has come to tell her the truth.

In her flat that evening, Duncan said, "Did Marcus say anything about the will, about Max leaving the money to you?"

"No. Not a word." She lifted her head drowsily from his shoulder. "It's probably something else he knew about before I did. Anyway, I don't think he's exactly hard up. He's got a suite in a hotel in Albemarle Street. By the way, I meant to say. He's invited us to dinner there on Thursday. I hope you can come."

"Why's he invited me? I've never met him."

"He asked me if there was anyone I wanted to bring. I said yes."

She sighed gently and buried her face again in Duncan's shoulder. They said nothing; they didn't need to. From the centre of the mantelpiece a peacock stood proud, alert, unmoving. It almost seemed to be watching them. A scuffed red box stood open on a small table by the wall. Inside the box was a silver brooch in the shape of a badger. In the light of the lamp its sapphire eye sparkled.